Welcome to the Funny Farm!
Gerri Allen

Life
on *and around*
The
FUNNY
F♦RM

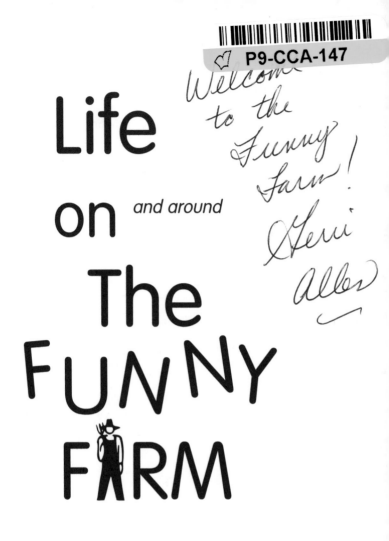

Gerri Powell Allen

FUNNY FARM, INK.

Milford, Michigan

Lyrics from the Green Acres theme song by Vic Mizzy
are © 1965, 1993 Vic Mizzy and used with permission.

Silhouette of Charles Trevor Allen by Joyce Redman
is © 2001 Joyce Redman and used with permission.

ISBN 0-9714971-0-9

Printed by Sheridan Books, Inc., a Sheridan Group Company
with offices in Ann Arbor and Chelsea, Michigan
and Fredericksburg, Virginia.
For more information, visit their website: www.sheridanbooks.com.

How to contact the author
(and her good-natured husband)
We'd love to hear from you. Share your reactions to a story. Drop Charley a condolence note! Order a copy of this book for a friend.
Send all correspondence to:
Funny Farm, INK.
P.O. Box 869
Highland, MI 48357

Acknowledgments

Thanks to readers of Funny Farm stories throughout the years. Your chuckles of appreciation, nods of recognition, and words of encouragement have kept me writing.

A special thanks to Bobbi Lamberson, Marge Lamberson, Bonnie Licari, Chris Miller, Janet Ochinero, Colleen O'Sullivan, Bill Powell, Sr., Nadine Russell, Alice Rose, Cheryl Taylor, Marge Truesdell and Nancy West for selecting the stories in this volume. You're the greatest.

Many thanks to Kay Wozniak for serving as my editor; I can always depend on your input and insight.

To members of the Achates Charter Chapter of the American Business Women's Association, this book would not have been possible without the affirmation you've freely given to me over the years. I owe you a debt I cannot repay.

To Chris and Dave Miller and the crew at Highland Feed and Water—thank you for allowing me to share these stories with your customers. And, thanks for taking a chance on an author wanna-be.

To my family—on both sides—thanks for your support and unconditional love. I couldn't have chosen better kin.

To Charley—my very best friend in the whole world—thanks, dear, you've been a great help and a good sport. But, it ain't over yet...

To all the unwitting volunteers—human and animal—who've been characters in Funny Farm stories, thanks for showing me how rich everyday life can be.

God bless you all!

Dedication

This book is dedicated to fellow procrastinators.
If a goal is a dream with a deadline—
don't wait—set a date!

Table of Contents

The Beginning

Dear Reader,

Life on the Funny Farm began for us in July 1991 when we bought seven acres and a century-old farmhouse. The plan was to fix up the old homestead, get married, sell Charley's house in Brighton and move to the farm. Then two months later, Charley's house burned down.

Although the order of our plans changed, we still managed to get married, sell Charley's house—after we rebuilt it—and move to the farm. The part that we haven't completed (and may never finish!) is fixing up the old homestead. As Charley says, we bought a 100-year-old house that's 90 years behind in maintenance. But, we love it.

Charley was raised on a farm in Ozark, Missouri. I was raised in Livonia—a Detroit suburb—and longed to live on a farm like mom did. So, when I found the five-bedroom farmhouse on seven acres, I knew it would be perfect for us. And, it is.

It's one-of-a-kind—like our relationship. That Ozark farm boy and Livonia city girl dated for 11 years before finally tying the knot. A second marriage for both of us—we wanted to make sure that we—like our farm—had a solid foundation.

The farm has been a haven for us and for Brad and Debbie—Charley's kids—who call me their *other* mother.

When they each needed a residence between college and marriage, they chose the farm. And, it's been here for the critters they brought with them and the ones they left behind! The farm, its residents and creatures provide plenty of writing fodder—sometimes to my family's chagrin. Charley often cringes when I sit down to write, knowing that he's a likely topic. (It's a great threat!!)

Charley is an engineer by training and a Renaissance man by nature. He can do just about anything I ask him to do...except maybe hand over the TV remote control! He's a whiz at computers and is my patient tech support.

Trained as a journalist and public relations specialist, I'm a writer by nature. Ever since Mr. Jungerman, my 9th grade English teacher, had us write our thoughts in a daily journal, I've been hooked. I worked on student newspapers, got my degree in journalism, became a newspaper reporter, then hired on as a school communicator.

In 1988, I began writing a monthly column for the newsletter of the local chapter of the American Business Women's Association (ABWA). It started out as general life observations and evolved into the Funny Farm adventures, which I'm still writing. For years, ABWA friends encouraged me to publish the columns. I said I would... someday.

In 1995, I offered my columns to Chris and Dave Miller, proprietors of Highland Feed and Water, when they began producing a regular store newsletter. The columns have appeared in it ever since. They, too, have encouraged me to publish these stories. I said I would... someday.

Well, someday is here! You have in your hands a collection of 35 columns—selected as favorites by several kind reviewers. I hope they bring a smile to your face or a fond memory to mind. And, if by chance you see yourself in some of our predicaments, you're not alone.

Sooner or later, we all visit The Funny Farm!

CHAPTER ONE

LOVING OTHERS

*Judge each day, not by
the harvest, but by the
seeds you plant.*

—Anonymous

Our wedding day

Ms. Geraldine Luella Powell wed Mr. Charles Verlyn Allen on Friday, August 14, 1992 at 6 p.m. The bride and groom exchanged their vows and rings under a blue and white canopy in the yard of their farm home in Milford.

The Rev. Edward Pedley, a family friend, officiated. The bride wore a pearl white, tea-length dress and the groom wore a dark suit.

The father of the bride gave her away. The mother of the groom played the bridal song and wedding march.

The children of the groom were the witnesses. During the period of reflection, Mrs. Charlotte Pedley sang a song entitled, "This is the Day."

The ceremony was followed by a catered meal under the canopy. It was a small, yet elegant wedding with 25 well-wishers in attendance.

After a brief honeymoon in the south, Mr. and Mrs. Allen will make their home in Milford....

September 2, 1992

Dear Family and Friends,

That's how the event might have been covered in the newspapers.

Now, here's the story behind the announcement.

Ms. Geraldine Luella Powell wed Mr. Charles Verlyn Allen on Friday, August 14, 1992 (we began planning for this in plenty of time—on Wednesday, July 29, 1992) **at 6 p.m.** (it was actually about 6:20 p.m.) **The bride and groom exchanged their vows and rings** (the rings arrived eight hours before the service, whew) **under a blue and white canopy** (owned and set up by a young man Charley used to coach, who now has young children of his own, who us old???) **in the yard of their farm home** (also known as the Funny Farm) **in Milford.**

The Rev. Edward Pedley, a family friend (Ed was Charley's pastor, Brad and Debbie grew up with the Pedley's children, and Ed's Uncle used to own the farm)**, officiated. The bride wore a pearl white, tea-length dress** (purchased one week before the occasion, Charley hoped it was something that could be worn again) **and the groom wore a dark suit** (his best and only).

The father of the bride gave her away (gladly, and made a lovely toast during the meal). **The mother of the groom played the bridal song and wedding march** (on the electronic keyboard she brought from Missouri. Charley's folks [Zelda and Marvin] came up to celebrate their 50th wedding anniversary on the 10th and helped us prepare for the wedding).

The children of the groom (and soon to be children of the bride) **were the witnesses.** (Neither one had been in a wedding before. They both held up pretty well—Brad a little better than Debbie...) **During the period of reflection, Mrs. Charlotte Pedley sang a song entitled, "This is the Day."** (She was a good sport about it, we asked her to sing about three days in advance.)

The ceremony was followed by a catered meal under the canopy. (Fresh, hot pizzas and Greek salad were delivered promptly at 7:30 p.m.). **It was a small** (we had talked about eloping, but Debbie wouldn't hear of it)**, yet elegant wedding** (thanks to Debbie for an excellent job of planning and decorating) **with 25 well-wishers in attendance.** (Guests included immediate family and two sets of friends, whom we put to work, one on the video camera and one on the 35 mm camera. Thanks to Brian and Rita Maust and Steve and Barb Altenberndt. We missed Charley's grandmother, his sister and brother-in-law and family, and my sister and brother-in-law and family. But we sent them a videotape.)

After a brief honeymoon in the south (okay, so we stayed at a hotel in Ann Arbor on our wedding night—Ann Arbor is south of Milford)**, Mr. and Mrs. Allen will make their home in Milford** (we are home and happy...).

So, that's our latest news. We figured this was too big to wait until our Christmas letter. And, we wanted you to read it here before it hit your local newspaper. We hope you and yours are healthy and happy. Thanks for being an important part of our lives.

Love,

      Gerri and Charley Allen
      (alias Mr. and Mrs. "A")

A letter to Lou

On Sunday, July 31, 1994, Luella Josephine Powell, my mom, passed away. She was nearly 82. Her funeral was Thursday, August 4, 1994. At her funeral, I read this letter on behalf of her five kids. I share it with you now, in her honor, for moms everywhere.

Mom,
You'll be happy to know that we really were paying attention to you all those years on Five Mile Road, on Mayfield Avenue, and even after we left home. And to prove it, the kids have listed some of the many things you taught us. Here's what we came up with.

You taught us:
--how to love one another
--and to take time out when we aren't feeling so loving.
--how to fall asleep anywhere, anytime,
    even while sewing.
--to sew.
--how to put babies (and even big people) to sleep
    by gently tracing circles on their faces.
--that it's important to do something right or not at all.

--to pay attention to detail.
--to have patience.
--to love our friends.
--to take pride in our workmanship.
--to be frugal with our money!
--to shop with coupons.
--to make the best macaroni and cheese in the world.
--to remember to pick up after ourselves.
--to always be there for family.
--how to make two pounds of steak feed a family of seven
   plus two guests.
--that it's important to enjoy life today because tomorrow
   might not come for us.
--to love unselfishly.
--how to take the little muscle out of an egg yolk and
   not break the yoke.
--how to put water in the ketchup bottle to get every
   last drop.
--how to paint window frames without getting paint
   on the windows or on ourselves.
--to have fun.
--to make killer banana nut bread.
--to work hard.
--to sit far away from the TV so we won't ruin our eyes.
   But, I think it's a little late for that, Mom.
--to love our spouses.
--that good things come in small packages.
--that we can do anything anyone else can do, and maybe
   even a little bit better.
--to help others in need.
--to wipe off the clothesline before we hang out the wash.
--that strawberry shortcake makes a great dinner on
   a summer Friday night.
--that women can be good drivers.

--to tell the truth.

--to repair things rather than throw them away.

--that broken limbs and broken hearts do mend.

--that dancing is an art form.

--to always do what's right

--to stick up for ourselves, but biting is not an acceptable
   way to do it.

--to love God.

--to always say our prayers.

--that you **can** win at solitaire without cheating.

--that it's important to enjoy and value your siblings.

--to conserve energy *"turn off those lights,*
   close that door" and

--to recycle before it was the popular thing to do.

--You taught us how to love children.

--And you taught us how to love ourselves.

For all of these reasons and many more, Mom,
we love you. And we just wanted to tell you one more time.

And the two shall become one...

This year, Charley and I have helped 12 couples celebrate nuptials—the coming together of two individuals into one union, one household, one home.

The weddings were as unique as the 24 individuals. Some were married in church, others were married in non-traditional settings like an art museum in Milwaukee, a dock on a lake in Michigan, a beach in Jamaica, a vineyard in Oregon, a cave in Missouri.

Some made their commitment in front of large crowds. Others had only the minister to witness their vows. Some had fancy celebrations immediately afterward with lots of fellowship, food and drink. Others waited a few weeks or months to hold more casual gatherings to toast their unions.

Some were doing this for the first time, like the young couple barely out of their teens—high-school sweethearts who had no other romantic history to speak of—bringing only themselves and their hopes and dreams to the union. Then there were the couples in their mid-to-late 20s, having loved and lost—short of the altar—bringing with them guarded hearts and cautious optimism. Some were promising to love, honor, and cherish for a second (or third) time knowing that these promises aren't easily kept.

Some were childless. Some would be welcoming a child soon and some were blending children from previous unions—children who may not have viewed the merger with the same dreamy-eyed excitement as the adults.

While all the couples were unique, met in different ways, had different kinds and lengths of courtships, and envisioned different futures, they all had the same idea. This was the one, the only, the last. No matter what had gone before, this was IT. This was their one, true love. They had found their soul-mate—someone with whom they discovered a cosmic connection.

It's their destiny to be together.

It's romantic.

It's storybook.

It's happily ever after.

In the marriage ceremony, two hearts and souls are joined willingly in an instant with an "I do" under the watchful eye of witnesses. The rest of the merger is accomplished gradually, carefully, over years with lots of dialogue sometimes with an "I do" and sometimes with a promise that "**I** won't ever **do** it again."

The wedding day is the easy part. The real test comes after the honeymoon when the soul-mates negotiate the finer points of the nuptial agreement like combining...

...two credit card balances, two eating habits, two sleeping cycles, two standards of cleanliness, two concepts of what is edible, two opinions on politics, two thoughts on where dirty socks should come to rest, two ways to manage money, two approaches to using electricity, two ideas about decorating (or not), two beliefs about the frequency of taking out the garbage, two systems for spending money, two views on where the new roll of toilet paper should go, two approaches to child rearing, two notions about what constitutes an essential expense, two concepts of what should be saved and what should be tossed, two answers to the questions: Are you hot, tired or hungry?, two positions on whether or not you really are lost and need to ask for directions, two reactions to the question: "What did you do with my _____ (fill in the blank: keys, watch, wallet, glasses, shoes, important papers)?," two theories about the correct place to squeeze the toothpaste tube, two opinions about the proper position of the toilet seat, two hypotheses about the ability of dirty dishes to grow legs and walk into the kitchen, two perceptions about what is considered a safe speed for channel surfing, two tastes in movies, two opinions about who was right, two interpretations of the phrase, "I won't be long," two concepts of what is a vegetable…

During these sometimes daily and sometimes delicate negotiations, the sweet soul-mate in you can be tempted to give way to alter egos: the troll mate, the droll mate or the I-want-control mate. You'll recognize him or her by an ugly look, a sharp tone, or a "my way or the highway attitude." If any of these should show up and start speaking for you, take evasive action immediately.

Stop. Breathe deeply. Find that wedding picture of you and your soul-mate—the one where you're gazing into each other's eyes as if no one else on earth existed. Look at that image. Remind yourself of what you agreed to do on your wedding day.

Remember it's your destiny to be together.

At times it's romantic.

At times it's storybook.

You have the power to make it happily ever after. Just remember that soul-mates don't always have to agree on the finer points…

…Two ideas on how to make a sandwich, two ways to say I'm sorry, two visions of the "perfect" birthday gift, two methods to express appreciation, two approaches to driving an automobile…

…two *thousand* ways to say I love you!

What's in a name?
(Ode to a new grandson)

With this age of information that emphasizes
   the younger generation and accommodates blended family,
Comes a question to the boomer generation
   whose children are now having babies:
How will I respond when called upon to be grandparentally?
And, what will this granddaughter or grandson,
   this new, little one, call me?"

As I sit in the hospital holding my step-grandson,
   Charles Trevor,
(The most perfect newborn baby I've seen just about ever.)
I discover I'm not immune to this age-old quandary.
I'm suddenly acting grandmotherly to the son of
   Kristin and Bradley.

A nurse on the floor of labor and delivery
   comments as she walks past me,
"Congratulations, what a proud grandmother you must be!"
"Why yes," I say happily, "I'm very proud to be
   his Grandma Number 3."
She smiles politely, continuing down the hall...
   (probably thinking I've lost it all).

She couldn't have guessed that in the grandparent best,
   Trevor is six-times blessed.
So, even though he's very small, when it comes
   to grandparents, Trevor stands quite tall.
His extended family includes Ed, Barb, Donna, Jerry,
   Charley and me.
So it's no wonder I query, what will Trevor call Grandma 3?

As we marvel over this new grandson,
   I'm not the only one asking this question.
We grandparents, oooh and aaah over this
   6 pound, 12 ounce miracle,
While working on grandparent handles—
   some really quite lyrical.

Brad's mom, Donna, decides on "Nonna Donna"—
   quite catchy.
While, Brad's dad, Charley, wonders when he got old enough
   to be *grandfatherly*.
Kristin's father, Ed, jokes that baby Trevor can call him "Leo."
As for me, I'm still wondering which is the best way to go.

There's no doubt that Charles *Trevor*
   will be called by his middle name.
Fifth in a line of males on Charley's side
   who's first name is the same.
While officially he's *"Trevor"* to friends and mom and dad,
The grandparents are busy thinking up monikers
   they might add.

To us, he's now Charley 5, Whatever Trevor, Mr. T.,
   Trev, Sweet Boy, Dude, Buddy,
   Munchkin, Bright Eyes and Cute T.
While thinking of nicknames for such a sweet one,
   it's fun to imagine all he'll become.

What about this small being who can mesmerize
   with a single coo?
What will his little voice sound like?
   What will he like to do?
What mischief will he get into?
   What will he need help out of?
What will be his favorite food?
   What kinds of books will he love?

Will he like baseball, music, bicycles, or soccer?
Will he be "into" motorcycles, trucks, basketball?
   Will he be a *rocker*?

Will he be a computer geek and learn to speak
   a language foreign to us?
Or will he be a nature boy who collects
   frogs and fireflies to show us?
Will he like to read and draw? Will he help his *ol' grandpa*?
Will he play with cats or dogs?
   Will he build things with Lincoln Logs?

Will he read the instructions or put it together
   by looking at the pieces?
Will he ask for directions or drive around
   until he doesn't know where he is?
Will he have a good sense of humor? A contagious laugh?
Will he be talkative? Will he enjoy hiking along a path?

Will he sing in the shower? Will he whistle while he works?
Will he have redeeming qualities and little endearing quirks?
Will he tell silly jokes or perform in front of a crowd?
Whoever he is, whatever he does,
   he's sure to make us proud!

And, whenever he needs any of us,
  he just has to call our name out loud:
      "Pop Pop, Grammy, Mamaw, Pepaw,
      Papa, Mommers, Pop or Memaw.
      Poppy, Gram, Gramps, or Granny,
      Paw Paw, Grandad, Popo, Nanny.
      Mimi, Grandpa, Grandma, Nana,
      Leo, Grand C, Nonna Donna."

Any noise his little voice sputters,
  any sound his little mouth utters,
The six of us will come to his aid.
That's, of course, why grandparents were made.

So, what will he call Grandma Number 3?
I guess it really doesn't matter much to me.

As I sit and watch in awe,
  as you coo for your third Grandma,
In that voice so sweet and small,
  I discover it doesn't matter at all.
I'll respond to you about anything, anytime you call.
Because, for you, no order is too big or too small.

To this miracle known as Charles Trevor,
  call me whatever you like, whenever.
I'm thrilled to be part of your life.
I plan to be around to meet
  your family and wife!

With love to you from me.
      Signed: Your Grandma Number 3.

CHAPTER TWO

LIKING CRITTERS

It's no coincidence that man's best friend cannot talk.

—Anonymous

Feeling a little sheepish...

I moved to a house in the country from my apartment in the city, so I could have animals. But, I was heart-broken after BB was hit and killed by a car in front of the house and so I announced, "No more dogs!"

That decree was in effect for six months, when, Abbey, a Golden Retriever puppy on her way to the pound, found us — with the help of Charley's son, Brad.

Then, nine months later, we decided Abbey needed a friend. That's when Sadie, a puppy with very large paws on her way to the pound, found us — again with Brad's help. Now Abbey is a year old and Sadie is four months old.

Abbey is 50 pounds of refined, gentle, purebred who loves Sadie. Sadie is 40 pounds of mutt energy — on her way to 80 pounds — who loves to play with Abbey.

Abbey, being true to her Retriever heritage, always has something in her mouth. And Sadie, being true to her puppy pedigree, always wants what Abbey has. This has led to many games of keep away as Abbey finds a scrap of cardboard, a Styrofoam cup or a plastic grocery bag that has blown onto our property and taunts Sadie with it. Sadie, with her uncoordinated legs, struggles to keep up with her "big sis" then decides the best strategy is to ambush Abbey and try to take the prized piece of litter away.

Sadie hasn't been too successful at taking away the object, but she's getting better at hanging on. Now the game is tug of war and the loser is usually me, having to pick up the litter that's been shredded into teeny, tiny pieces and strewn on the ground.

These contests have been the highlight of our daily walks over the last few months. The dogs are getting a good romp and I'm getting stooping and bending exercise as I collect the remnants of their struggle. And, my reflexes are improving. I'm getting faster at intervening before the shredding begins. It really is great fun and I marvel at how being with these two, after a crazy day at work, puts things into perspective.

Last night, it was my turn to walk "the girls" and, as usual, the keep away games began as soon as they were out of the gate. This time it was Sadie who threw down the gauntlet, grabbing the sour cream container I use for a dog food scoop and racing down the lane.

To Sadie's dismay, Abbey wasn't paying much attention. Abbey ran ahead of us and out of view. Sadie carried the container for a little while, but it quickly became a burden, since no one else was interested in it. She dropped it in the field and went to look for Abbey.

We found Abbey at the end of the property, carefully eyeing the neighbor's herd of sheep that had wandered down to our end of the fence. One of the ewes noticed Abbey and started walking toward her. Abbey, in turn, cautiously approached the fence. Their noses touched. Both of them sniffing curiously.

I stood still, talking calmly to the sheep while Sadie paced nervously near me. Soon, the rest of the herd quietly came to where the dog and ewe were sniffing, to see what was happening. One little one even stood up on her hind legs and balanced herself on the rear end of another to see above the crowd. I stood there kicking myself for not having my camera and attempted to etch the image in my mind.

As the crowd moved closer to the fence, Abbey became frightened and broke the nose-to-nose connection. She looked at me, then looked back at the sheep as if to say, "What kind of dogs are they?"

About that time, the herd lost interest and began moving toward the barn. The one, brave ewe also began to ease away.

By this time, Sadie was beside herself, beckoning us to continue the walk. "Okay, okay," I said, turning back toward the house. But, Abbey stayed at the fence, watching the sheep. I called to her several times before she responded. Then, Sadie appeared with the sour cream container and the chase was on.

The rest of our walk was uneventful — except that the sour cream container got lost someplace in the field. And, I wondered if the encounter at the fence had made an impression on Abbey.

This morning, I bundled up and took the girls for their morning walk, hoping to find the sour cream container. Instead, I found Abbey at the end of our property, sniffing the ground where the encounter had taken place yesterday.

I went up to her and said, "The sheep aren't here Abbey, they're sleeping." Then I looked down and saw a plastic bag on the other side of the fence. "Silly me," I said. "You don't care about those sheep. You just want that plastic bag so you can play keep away from Sadie.

"You can't have it. Com'on, let's go..."

As I walked away, Abbey lingered, looking up from the ground and gazing down the fence row toward the barn. Curious, I followed her gaze.

Why, she wasn't interested in the plastic bag at all.

There, down at the end of the fence row, stood the herd of sheep!

Bats in the belfry?

It was after work. I had taken my glasses off downstairs and walked upstairs to get changed. As I entered our room, I looked down at the floor by my dresser and saw something. Without my glasses, it looked like a blurry blob.

Since everything far away looks like a blurry blob without my glasses, I had to get really close before I discovered it was a *live*, blurry blob. It was a bat.

We've had bats upstairs before, so I was prepared. Quickly I found the bat catcher (an old ice cream bucket), carefully placed it over the critter and sat a heavy flashlight on top of the bucket. I thought about sliding a piece of cardboard underneath him, trapping him and ushering him outside, as we do all intruders from the animal and insect world, but decided instead to wait for Charley to get back from his church softball game. He could have the honor.

As I walked back into the hallway, I noticed something hanging out from a crack in the ceiling. Again, without my glasses, I could barely make it out. As I struggled to get it in focus, it moved. I ran downstairs, donned my glasses, grabbed a flashlight and ran back upstairs. I shone the flashlight on the thing hanging out of the ceiling and it eventually moved again. It was the head of a small bat and he was looking at me. I studied him for a minute then decided to leave him for Charley, too.

When Charley came home an hour later, I greeted him at the door and told him of our house guests. He wasted no time, and headed directly upstairs.

He scooped up the first bat that I had left under the ice cream container and took him outside for release. I held the door open and made sure our cat, Wolfie, didn't follow. I waited to hear the results.

Charley called to me and when I went over to him, I noticed the ice cream bucket still had a resident. "Look, he's just a baby," Charley said. I peered into the bucket and there he lay — a tiny, fragile, furless, flightless creature. "If I let him go, he won't survive the night," Charley noted.

So, there we stood, both studying this little bat baby. He was tiny and had no fur. His skin was gray and wrinkly. His underbelly was a soft pink. His ears were oversized, giving him a Dumbo-like quality. His wings were tissue paper thin. His wide feet each had five stubby toes that gripped the cardboard tightly. He was helpless. What should we do with him?

Unsure, we rummaged around for a temporary home to put him in. As Charley punched air holes in the lid, I watched the little fellow flop around in the bottom. He seemed to be looking for something. Then I saw his mouth open and his tongue lick the sides and then bottom of the container. I was fascinated. Every once in a while, he would look up as if to say, "Hey, can't you see I'm thirsty?"

Taking the hint, I got some milk from the frig, warmed it in the microwave and gently placed a few drops on the bottom of the container, next to Elmer Thud's mouth. (It was Charley's idea to name him Elmer. I added the "Thud" to imitate the sound he must have made when he fell out of the ceiling.)

While, I stayed downstairs monitoring Elmer, Charley went upstairs to check on his sibling. I continued to watch Elmer, talking to him, encouraging him to try some of the milk. It wasn't mom's milk, but hey, it was wet. He didn't seem interested, in fact, all of a sudden he lay motionless. I couldn't see him breathing,

So, I tapped on the side of the container and he acted like he was waking up. He'd lift his head, then let it drop back down. And, he hadn't taken a drink. He seemed to stop breathing several times and each time I'd tap on the container, he'd revive. "If you would only take a drink, I'm sure you'd feel better," I coaxed.

Charley came back into the kitchen, announcing that he had pushed Elmer's sibling back into the ceiling and that's what we needed to do with Elmer. "We've got to get him back to his mother, it's his only chance," Charley said.

"I don't know if he's gonna make it," I said. "He seems pretty weak and he hasn't tried any of the milk." He must have heard us talking. To prove me wrong, he awoke from his stupor and began licking the milk.

He polished off the original supply and began searching the bottom for more. So, I placed a few more drops in front of his face and he lapped them up. At one point, he held his head up, exposing a milk mustache and beard around his miniature mouth. He was actually kind of cute.

Just as I was starting to get attached to him, Charley said it was time to help Elmer rejoin his family. So, we took Elmer upstairs, laid him on a flat piece of cardboard and Charley moved him close to the opening where his sibling had just been. Without any more help than that, Elmer scurried into the opening and out of sight.

Charley took a piece of wood, covered the opening and secured it with wood screws, (using his cordless electric drill, of course). "There, that should take care of that," Charley said. "Bye Elmer," I said. "Maybe we'll see you when you're old enough to fly."

Two months later: As I was going upstairs to bed, I looked up and saw a full grown bat soaring close to the ceiling. [The folks at the Cooperative Extension Service tell us this usually happens in late August when the young bats, who are finally old enough to fly, try to make their way outside at night and occasionally take a wrong turn.]

So, I called for reinforcements, "Hey, Charley, I think Elmer has come back to visit us." Charley went upstairs, trapped the wayward bat in the ice cream container, then turned him loose outside where he was supposed to be.

We've been co-existing with bats ever since we moved to the farm. We want to have them around the farm but not in the house. So, we've done our homework to be good hosts. We've read about them, talked to the experts about them, and even built a deluxe bat house for them. Yet, they still won't stay outside where they belong. That means our next challenge will be to make our house bat-proof.

Until then, we'll continue to catch the wayward few and release them outside. Some people say we're crazy — that we should "do away with the bats" instead of catching them and turning them loose outdoors. I wonder what Elmer would say?

Midnight marauders

It was 2:30 Sunday morning and I had gotten up to use the facilities. While in the bathroom, I heard a commotion out on the deck. It sounded as if someone had lost his or her footing and had fallen off. I didn't hear the dogs bark and wondered how he or she had gotten past our natural, early warning system.

Now completely awake, I quietly, carefully walked to the side door and peeked out. I grabbed a nearby yardstick, ready for whatever I might face.

As my eyes adjusted to the dim moonlight, I was able to make out one, two, three, four intruders. They were young. I could tell because they weren't worried about keeping their activities a secret. In fact, they were so engrossed in what they were doing, they didn't even notice me watching them. They were having a free-for-all on our deck in the middle of the night!

At first, I was worried about the cats. Were they in any danger? But, I didn't see any of them and the only things around their house — the six-room, three-level cat condo — were the juveniles.

Then I was worried about our belongings. These rowdies were rambling all over the deck.

They didn't seem interested in the gas grill. I was relieved about that. But I was afraid — with all the horseplay that was going on — that one of them would get hurt and we'd hear from their parents.

And, then there was the mess they were making. They'd spilled the cats' water. They'd overturned the food bowls. They had moved the outdoor thermometer. And, there were muddy footprints everywhere.

I thought about waking Charley and then I recognized the intruders as belonging next door. Once I determined there was no real danger, I decided to act.

I banged the yardstick on the window and yelled. "Hey you, get out of here!" They paused, looked up defiantly in my direction, and returned to their rough housing.

So, I turned on the porch light, but that didn't phase them either. They continued to romp around, as if they were alone.

Even though the light didn't scare them away, it did help me get a better look at them. "Why you're much younger than I thought," I said out loud. "In fact, you're so little I'd guess you're really just pups."

I watched as two of them stayed on the ground while the other two moved to the upstairs of the cat condo, stretching their little bodies so their feet could reach the next level. Once on the upper level, they moved in and out of each room checking out every corner.

For a moment, I was entertained by all the mischief. I hadn't ever been this close to such small raccoons. Then I reminded myself that these are **wild** raccoons wreaking havoc on **my** deck.

"I don't care how cute you are, you can't continue this nonsense around here. You give me no choice," I said.

And, I swung open the door intending to scare them away. Instead, they came running curiously toward the open door. I had to hurry to close it before they got into the house.

Since I couldn't scare them away. I decided to relax and enjoy watching them. Like typical kids, they were messy, curious, and full of energy. They climbed and rolled and crawled around the deck. They tried to get into every hole they could find. Often their curiosity stretched further than their short legs, and they'd end up tumbling to the ground. I knew no one was hurt, because they were making purring and cooing sounds.

In the midst of all this, one became fascinated by a moth that had been circling the porch light. He sat on his haunches and tried to catch it between his little hand-like paws. The moth eventually flew too high, and the raccoon had stretched as far as he could before losing his balance and interest.

At one point during the frivolity, I tapped on the storm door and two of the pups came over to it. I stuck my face against the window and said "Boo! You're supposed to be afraid of me." Instead the two of them pressed their little faces against the window to get a better look inside!

While they took note of me, I studied them. They each had a black mask like the Lone Ranger, a shiny black nose, pointed ears, a ringed tail, very soft-looking fur, and those nimble paws. These were very cute although very raucous critters.

Soon they lost interest in me. The few morsels of cat food had been eaten, all the nooks and crevices had been explored, and a new adventure called.

So, the four crawled down off the deck and, without saying good-bye, waddled off into the woods nearby.

After all this excitement, I decided it was time to go back to bed. I turned off the porch light, put up the yardstick, and headed for the sack.

But I was more wide awake than I had first thought. It took me a little while to settle in. To help in the process as I drifted off to sleep, I counted raccoons instead of sheep.

Our little oasis

It may not be "House Beautiful," but this old farmhouse — and the seven acres on which it sits — is our oasis. When life gets crazy, it's a comforting place to be. And, that's the very place I was headed last Tuesday night, after working late.

It was after dusk and my drive home from the city takes me through some areas that are heavily traveled by deer and other wildlife. With hunting season here, I was being extra cautious as I moved along the wooded two-lanes, reminding myself to *watch for deer.*

As I turned down our road, I felt relieved that the drive was almost over. I was tired and wanted to be home. As I pulled in, my high beams flooded the driveway and I noticed Charley's truck was gone. He had already left for his ballgame.

Then my headlights hit the grass next to the garage and two sets of glowing eyes shown back. *What the heck is that?* I wondered. *Are they deer? No. They were too small. Our dogs? No. They were still in the pen.* They appeared to be two Springer Spaniels that I had never seen before. *Were they friendly? Should I get out of the car?*

I rolled down my window and began talking to them. "Hi guys, what are you doing here?" No response, they just continued to lay on the ground and look at me with those eyes.

By now our dogs were barking and carrying on about these intruders. I assured them that it was O.K. and reassured myself that it was safe to get out of the car. I continued to talk to the pair as I exited the car and entered the back door of the house. They didn't move.

I unloaded my work stuff, listened to phone messages, read Charley's note that said he hadn't had time to walk the dogs and changed into my dog-walking clothes. I hoped the Spaniels had moved on to explore other territories, so I could walk "the girls" in peace. I looked out the window toward the garage and didn't see them. *Good*, I thought. *They're gone.*

I put on my jacket and boots and scooped out a bowl of dog food for Abbey and Sadie. As I went to open the back door, I rediscovered the Spaniels. One was laying against the back door and the other was staring up at me with those eyes. I noticed they had on collars, so that told me they belonged to someone. But, I've learned enough about animals not to make any assumptions about their friendliness.

I needed to walk my dogs and these dogs were obviously not going anywhere anytime soon. What to do? Then I got an idea.

I cracked open the back door and stuck the food bowl out. "Are you guys hungry?" In a flash, the bigger of the two began eating. The smaller one hesitated, that's when I noticed he had an I.D. tag.

Now I had my plan. I eased out the back door holding the food bowl low, being careful not to startle them. Then I led them down toward the garage. "I bet you guys are thirsty, too. If you come inside here, I'll give you plenty of food and water, just follow me."

It worked! They followed me into the garage and I put the food on the floor. By now, their entire attention was on eating. While the smaller one ate, I studied his tag. His name was Rocky and his owner's phone number was etched at the bottom. I read the number several times until I knew it.

I closed the dogs in the garage and repeated the phone number as I ran to the house. I dialed the number and a man answered the phone. By now it was nearly 9 p.m.

"Hi," I said, "Uh...I think I have your dogs in my garage." "My dogs?" he asked. "Are they two brown and white Springer Spaniels? Their names are Rex and Rocky."

When he said Rocky, I knew I had the right person. "Yup, that's them," I said. I gave him my phone number and directions to our house and he said, "We'll be there in about ten minutes."

I went back out to the garage and gave the runaways some water. About ten minutes later, a white car pulled up in the driveway and a man and women got out. I opened the garage door and Rex and Rocky excitedly greeted their owners.

While they rejoiced in finding each other, the husband told me he had last seen them on Sunday when he was cleaning out their pen. He let the dogs out to stretch their legs for a few minutes while he talked with a neighbor and the dogs took off. "With this being hunting season, we thought maybe someone had seen them along the road and picked them up," he said.

"They really came a long way," the wife explained. "We live more than seven miles from here. Rex is ten years old and Rocky, my daughter's dog, is only one. We were beginning to think we'd never see them again."

She offered to give me something for the long distance phone call and the food, but my reward was seeing how happy everyone was. I told them that they could return the favor to someone else one day.

So, they loaded the dogs in the car and I waved as they pulled out of the driveway. Then I went for a moonlight walk with "the girls."

When Charley came home, he asked me if I had seen "those two Springer Spaniels laying in the grass by the garage."

"Oh yes," I smiled. "Word is out about our little oasis..."

I've been waiting for you.

She was weak, listless and refused even a small drink of water, so we rushed her to emergency.

Her breathing was labored all the way to the hospital. Yet she still mustered the energy to complain. On the way, I had assured her the doctor would fix her up as good as new.

But now I wasn't so certain.

We left her overnight and the doctor said her temperature had gotten back to normal by 4 a.m. this morning. That was good. They put her on an IV to hydrate her. Now, she was full of liquid, but there was no evidence that her kidneys were functioning. That was bad.

In her update, the doctor called her condition "grave." We gave permission to try more aggressive diuretics, if that failed our only alternative was to take her to Lansing for kidney dialysis followed by a transplant and there was no guarantee of success....

Not sure what to do, we prayed and decided to wait 24 hours to see if the aggressive treatment would work. We couldn't imagine losing her...

More dog than cat, Nakima, the tiny calico who came to the farm five years ago by way of Charley's daughter, Debbie, had become part of the family. Debbie rescued her from the pound and at first she cowered and hid from us. We suspected she'd been abused.

We bided our time and gradually she began to trust us. She lived outdoors, spending her evenings in a house enclosed in a pen and her days roaming free on the property. She was never very far away and was always full of meow commentary, making her seem more human than feline.

At night, she'd always return from prowling the grounds to have dinner and be put to bed. She'd lead you to her pen, meowing as she went, as if to say, "It's about time you got here. I've been waiting for you."

But, that Friday night she didn't come home. I called to her, got no response and said, "If that's the way you want to be, you'll just have to go without dinner." I left her pen open and as I went inside, I felt a twinge of worry but assured myself that she'd be waiting for breakfast at daybreak.

On Saturday I walked our dogs, Abbey and Sadie, but saw no evidence of Nakima. I went to several of her favorite spots and called to her, listening for that ever present, back-talking meow. Silence. I checked the garage, the barn, and the shed. Nothing.

Saturday night, I asked Charley to keep an eye out for her when he walked the girls at dusk. Surely she'd be hungry and return home by then. No Nakima.

The temperature reached the mid-90s on Saturday and the weather forecast predicted a scorcher for Sunday, too. On Sunday, we spent even more time looking for her. Was she trapped somewhere? Was she hurt? Did she dart in front of a car? We looked along the side of the road as we drove to church. Thankfully, we saw no Nakima.

Sunday night came and went and Nakima was still AWOL. Charley admitted that even he was beginning to worry and that made me worry more.

By Monday morning, I was in a funk. Would I ever know what happened to her? I knew she'd try to get home if she could. As I walked the girls, I prayed for her return.

After dark on Monday night, Charley was tinkering with the used lawn tractor we had just purchased. He was working on the engine and needed me to start and stop it quickly, so he could locate the source of the squealing noise. I was sitting in the mower seat, cranking the engine then turning it off.

The third time that he listened carefully to the engine squeal and cough to a stop, I heard a different kind of cough. I turned in the mower seat to see something move by the base of Nakima's favorite tree, followed by a deep, congested cough and a faint meow. Could it be?

I jumped off the mower and ran to the small, dark figure. My prayers were answered. It was Nakima! She'd come home. I scooped her up and was about to scold her when I realized she was very weak. Charley was amazed that I had heard her amidst the tractor noise. He followed me into the house.

Upon closer examination, it was obvious she needed to get to the vet. By now it was 10:30 p.m. I called the emergency animal hospital down the road and said we were on our way. Charley helped load her in the car.

At first, I was afraid it was Feline Leukemia. I'd seen it devastate other cats and knew the sad, inevitable outcome. But the emergency vet didn't mention it as a possibility. They would treat her for the upper respiratory symptoms. "It didn't look too bad." So, we left her there overnight. My heart was lighter as we drove home.

But by the next morning, they were looking at an elevated white blood cell count and possible kidney failure. They asked if she had ingested any toxins like anti-freeze. We knew she didn't have access to that sort of thing at the farm. That's when Charley guessed that she may have wandered into a neighbor's garage and been locked in when they left town over the very hot weekend. She could have been really thirsty and out of desperation drunk something toxic.

…Unfortunately we saw no improvement after our 24-hour wait. The aggressive treatment seemed to have no effect. Little Nakima was struggling to keep her eyes open and she was unable to get comfortable because of the fluid build up in her tiny body. We decided to try one last powerful drug to get some kidney function and stayed with her until it had more than enough time to work. Still no response.

We'd run out of viable options. She was barely hanging on. That's when we decided it was time to say goodbye. She'd had a good life and added much joy to ours. We signed the release form, told her she was a good girl, left the room and the vet gave her one last injection. Nakima was gone in minutes.

Back home, we held a memorial service and laid her to rest under a tree out in our field.

Now she's home where she belongs—never far away.

And, on still mornings, if you listen closely as you pass by the spot, you can hear her meow, "It's about time you got here. I've been waiting for you."

A little bird told us

On that Wednesday night Charley's golf league had finished a few hours before mine, so he had time to walk the dogs and eat dinner before I got home about 9:30. I had no sooner hit the back door than Charley asked me to grab a flashlight and follow him outside.

Excitedly, he led me to the rabbit hutch that sits behind our garage. The hutch was a cast-off that we inherited because, on the farm, we had the space to store it. But, it never had an occupant – until now.

Charley directed me to "shine the flashlight inside the hutch." As I did, two eyes shone in the light. "What have you got in there?" I asked. "A rabbit? "No, look closer," he said.

As my eyes adjusted to the darkness, the creature looking back at us gradually became visible. "It's a pigeon." Charley announced proudly.

"I see that. How did she get in there?" I asked.

"I picked her up with my bare hands and put her in. I don't think she can fly and she seemed to know I'd help her," he said.

Charley first saw her when he drove into the driveway after golf. She was perched on a piece of lumber that was leaning against the garage door. He tried to shoo her away before he let the dogs out to go for a walk but she didn't budge. So he put her in the hutch for safekeeping. He gave her some water and made a nest by putting some straw in a small plastic tub.

"She's probably hungry. Do we have anything to feed her?" he wondered.

"I have some wild birdseed that was given to me. I bet she'd like that." I said.

So we fed the pigeon, named her "Sweetie Bird" and said good night. The next morning when I went out to check on her, she'd eaten some birdseed and was drinking water from her bowl.

We checked the encyclopedia and it confirmed that we were doing the right things for Sweetie. It told us that pigeons eat fruit and seeds and that they're one of the few groups of birds that can drink with their bills by sticking them in the water and sucking. Armed with this information, we decided to keep Sweetie at the farm while she convalesced.

After closer examination, we discovered that Sweetie's wing was injured, that's why she couldn't fly. But she seemed to trust us and began responding to the care that we were giving her. Soon we fell into a routine with our winged guest.

Charley would check on her at night. And, each morning I'd refresh Sweetie's water and give her more birdseed. We even made a special trip to our favorite feed store to get some bird supplies like a cuddle bone to dull her beak (and save our fingers) and some gravel to help with her digestion.

At first, she watched from her nest as I performed the daily ritual of putting seed in her bowl, gravel in a second bowl and water in the bowl that she used for drinking and bathing. (We learned quickly to make sure all her bowls were weighted and unable to be tipped.) As she grew stronger, she'd venture from her nest and stand near the bowls as I replenished them, studying me out of one or the other of her eyes.

After a couple of weeks, Sweetie was now starting to make warning noises if I'd get too close as I fed and watered her. Then one morning she started to peck at me as I reached in for her bowl.

Although I assumed it meant she was feeling better, I wasn't happy about a wild bird attacking the hand that was feeding her. Fortunately, she had bad aim. By now I was feeding her with the hutch door wide open but she showed no interest in leaving.

Every morning when I walked toward Sweetie's hutch, I'd wonder if she'd survived the night and would be relieved when I'd see her two beady eyes watching me. But one morning I walked out to find the bottom of the hutch covered in blood. My heart sank as I rushed to her nest expecting the worst.

To my relief, she was alive but bleeding from her foot where she had lost one of her toenails. Thankfully, after a while the bleeding stopped, and after two days a new nail had grown in its place.

After the bloody toenail incident, we decided it was time to see if Sweetie would fly. So, Charley put on some gloves to protect his hands (Sweetie's aim was improving), extracted her from the hutch, and placed her on its roof. We were encouraged as she stretched her wings, flapped them and hopped about three feet onto the garage roof — where she remained. She paced nervously zigzagging her way to the roof's peak. But she never flapped her wings.

At that point, Charley crawled onto the roof to help Sweetie with her send off. But, every time he moved toward her, she'd strut the other way, bobbing her head and high stepping but never moving her wings. It was clear that Sweetie was feeling better as she dodged Charley at every turn. He finally herded her back toward the ground, grabbed her and placed her back in the hutch.

"Her reflexes are pretty good, but I don't think she's ready to fly yet." Charley announced, trying to catch his breath.

I wondered if Sweetie was ever going to leave us. In a few weeks we'd be traveling to Missouri on business and I worried if we'd find someone to care for her while we were gone. "You need to fly away before we go away," I told Sweetie after the garage incident.

The next few mornings when I'd feed Sweetie, she'd walk to the edge of the cage and peer out the open door but never made an attempt to leave the hutch. Then on that Saturday, 14 days before our scheduled departure to Missouri, she pecked at me and batted my hand several times with what used to be her bad wing. I laughed and reminded her that she was running out of time.

That afternoon as I was working in the basement I heard Charley exclaim from the backyard, "Sweetie's flown the coop!" I ran outside but was too late to see her fly away.

Charley had gone out to check on her and she was flying around in the hutch crashing into one side and then the other. "I was afraid she was going to hurt herself, so I opened the hutch door. She moved to the open door, looked out and flew away," he explained.

I was sad that I hadn't seen her take off, yet I was relieved that she was back on her own. But with two weeks before we left for Missouri, she could have hung around a little longer. I guess she had her reasons.

The next day, Sunday, we got a call telling us that Charley's 96-year old grandmother who lived in Missouri was ill and by Tuesday we were on our way to Missouri for Grandma's funeral – leaving twelve days earlier than we had planned.

The trip surprised everyone – everyone except Sweetie.

How lucky can you get?

It was Tuesday night and I had just come in from work. It was past nine and I was glad to be home. I was looking forward to watching my favorite TV sitcom and then going to bed.

I had just kicked off my shoes when Charley raced into the room, handed me a flashlight and beckoned me to follow him outside. "Now?" I moaned. "But, I'm in my good clothes. Shouldn't I at least put on my boots?" "No," he said already out the door. "It's not far."

So, off he went and I hurried to catch up, still wearing my dress, nylons and street shoes. We passed the garage and headed for the barn. We passed the barn and continued toward the field. Now, I was beginning to get miffed. "How much further is it? If I knew we were coming out this far, I'd have put on a coat. It's cold out here," I complained.

"It's not much further," he said and began to walk into the tall grass. "In here," he motioned with the flashlight. "I can't go in there," I protested. "Those pricker bushes will run my nylons. I'm staying right here. Why did you bring me out here, anyway?" "You'll see," he said, and began using the flashlight to search the area, moving its beam back and forth, illuminating the field grass and scrub trees in its path.

"It's right over here, I know it," Charley said confidently. While he was concentrating on the search, I was concentrating on the cold night air that was penetrating my thin work clothes. Knowing that once he puts his mind to something he doesn't give up, I figured it was better to help look rather than stand and complain. So, I dodged the pricker bushes and began to shine my light, too.

"OK. So now that you have me in here, what am I looking for?" I asked more insistently than the last time.

"It was right over here," Charley said. "I could have sworn it was by this small tree. But, it looked different in the daylight."

"Let me put it to you another way," I said, fighting a shiver. "If I knew what I was looking for, I could tell you if I found it!"

"Well, okay," he said. "I thought I could find it easily but since I can't, why don't you go inside, get changed and bring out the big flashlight. And, then I'll tell you."

I was glad to be dismissed, if only for a few minutes. I made my way back to the house, changed into my farm clothes, put on a field coat, grabbed a coat for Charley, picked up the big flashlight (the one that has a bulb the size of a car headlight), slipped on my boots, and returned to the field where the beam from Charley's flashlight continued to slice through the darkness.

"Now will you tell me what we're looking for?"

"A rabbit's nest," he said.

It seems when he was walking the dogs earlier in the evening, Abbey (our Golden Retriever) carried one of the rabbits from its nest and deposited it in the path where Charley came upon it. With Sadie, our rabbit-hunter mutt, close behind, Charley scooped up the small, partially developed, unhurt bunny whose eyes were still closed and temporarily put him in the old rabbit hutch behind the garage for safekeeping while he finished feeding the dogs.

Then he retrieved the bunny, walked back to the field where we were now standing and deposited him in the rabbit's nest he easily found in the daylight. "It's got to be right here by this tree," he said. "It's a hole and it's filled with lots of rabbit fur to keep him warm. If we find the rabbit fur, we've found the nest."

We did find a few wisps of rabbit fur in the vicinity of where Charley thought the nest should be – but no hole and no bunny. After more than an hour of tromping around in the same few feet of grass, I was growing weary of the search. Besides, not only was my favorite TV program long over, it was past my bedtime.

After pleading my case, Charley agreed to let me go in the house. I left the dark field noting that the search's intensity was growing as the beam of light darted around the field with urgency.

After only five minutes in the house, Charley called to me from outside. "I found it," he said. "It was in the very spot we were looking. The mama rabbit just did a great job of covering up the hole. Come and see."

I agreed to go out to the field one last time to see his discovery. Charley had marked it with some tissue, so this time it was easy to find. First, he peeled back the protective cover of grass the mother rabbit had placed over it. Then he put his finger in the hole and parted the layer of two-inch thick rabbit fur that was lining the nest, exposing a little rabbit belly.

"See he's in there," Charley said. "I knew it was right here by this tree."

After we confirmed that he was okay, we covered up the rabbit's nest. We'd need to protect the little guy from our dogs, who on their daily walk, might try to dig him up. We figured Sadie had probably already dined on his siblings.

So, every morning and every evening before we'd walk the dogs, we'd put a wash tub over the top of the nest and remove it once the girls were inside their pen. "If we can keep the dogs away from him until he's a little older, he might have a chance," Charley said. "It shouldn't be too much longer before his mama moves him."

Sure enough, the following Saturday, when I went out to cover up the rabbit's nest with the wash tub, the grass that had been camouflaging it was peeled back. And the rabbit's fur that had been so carefully packed around the baby bunny was sitting on top of the grass, revealing an empty nest. The bunny and his mother were gone. We had done all we could. Now it was up to nature to do the rest.

As I looked down at the empty nest, I thought about the baby rabbit and then about the man who had become his protector, never giving up on finding him.

I hoped the baby bunny knew how lucky he was to have Charley for a friend.

Any dumb bunny could figure that out.

What a stinker!

It's 7 a.m. on a peaceful June morning. Sunshine. Gentle breeze. Low 50s. Dew on the grass. Flowering trees in bloom.

The girls, Abbey, a 55-pound Golden Retriever, and Sadie, a 90-pound mixed breed, wait patiently for me to open the gate of their pen. It's time for their morning walk. I open it and they burst out. They run to the front of the house sniffing for evidence of trespasser canines so they can play their game of pee tag. I head for the property out back. We leave much of our seven acres natural to give the local wildlife refuge. We mow mainly around the house and cut walking paths out back.

I enter one of the mowed paths. The four-foot tall grasses bend gracefully over the three-foot wide path forming a natural archway that I could walk under if I were two feet tall. Instead, I plow through the arched greenery parting it with my knees, rustling as I go.

Soon, Abbey gallops by, whooshing through the grasses, passing me on the left. Sadie is still behind us. She soon lumbers by, brushing my right leg, pushing back the long grass in her way.

I take a deep breath, thankful that I live in the country, where the air is rich with the sweet aroma of flowering trees, fresh cut hay, wildflowers, and…skunk?…

"Did you get a whiff of that?" I ask Sadie (who has now assumed her usual spot by my side). The distinctive aroma seems to move with us down the path. "Well, Sadie, I hope Abbey isn't wearing that scent." (I haven't seen her since she first galloped by me.)

I reach the end of our property and greet the neighbors' sheep, goats and donkey as I do everyday. "Good morning everyone. Good morning!"

I make the turn and start across the back path. The skunk scent is stronger now and I see Abbey, pawing at something in the grass. I hurry toward her with Sadie in pursuit. The closer I get, the stronger the skunk smell gets. Abbey definitely got sprayed. Continuing to paw in the grass, she looks up at me as if to say, "See what I found?" I peer over the tall grass and spy a small, creature trying to make itself less obvious by not moving. It has a black fur coat, a black bushy tail and a white stripe painted on its back – a baby skunk.

Abbey continues pawing at the skunk's hindquarters. I think she wants the little guy to run so she can chase him. "No, Abbey!" I scold. "Leave him alone!" Abbey backs off. That creates the opening for Sadie—legendary rabbit hunter. Before I can move, Sadie lunges into the tall grass and plucks the baby skunk out by the scruff of his neck – much like a cat would grab a kitten – and gallops down the path toward the house. If she makes it back to the pen, there's no hope for the little guy.

I run after her hollering and waving my arms, "No Sadie! Drop it!!" It isn't looking good. I've seen this action before. Sadie doesn't voluntarily surrender her prey.

I don't know if my flailing arms and desperate commands startle her or if Sadie doesn't like the taste of skunk. No matter, she drops the little fella right in the middle of the path.

I hurry toward him. And there we are. Two dogs circling a baby skunk frozen in fear and a city gal hovering over him waving her arms to keep the dogs at bay.

"Now what?" I ask aloud. "Pick him up and carry him to safety," I answer. Fortunately because of the cool morning, I was wearing gloves. I could pick him up and even if he tried to bite me, I'd be protected. But what about that little spray apparatus. Hopefully, he didn't have time to reload after spritzing Abbey.

Dogs circling. Skunk surrounded. No time to waste. I reach down with both hands, gently place my fingers under him and begin to lift. I feel resistance. Is he holding on to the grass?

Chunky little critter. I bring him carefully toward me. Dogs jumping up to see him. His tiny body fits in the palm of my right hand. His chin rests in the pocket between my thumb and forefinger. He's breathing through his mouth. His black eyes are studying me. I do a quick survey for damage. No blood. No visible marks of trauma, except for some dog saliva.

"Are you okay, little buddy?" His miniature paws have tiny, long, pointed claws. The right front paw is wrapped around the outside of my thumb. The left front paw is curled around the outside of my forefinger. He seems to be hanging on. I stroke the top of his little head and cup my left hand over my right to give him some protection. He doesn't move.

I start walking back toward the house. The dogs follow, still interested in what my hands contain. Sadie stays closer than usual. As we walk, I examine the little fella's soft, black fur; the white stripe that splits in two about three-fourths of the way down his back; his tiny ears; his jet black eyes and nose; his pink tongue visible as he continues to pant. I wonder if he's still nursing. I hope he can take care of himself.

We're halfway back now, close to where we saw those two adult skunks a few weeks ago. "What am I going to do with you?" I ask the little guy. For a moment, I contemplate keeping him. Then I remember that I have to go to work today.

Taking advantage of my inattention, he makes his move and flips over on his back, exposing what I guess to be his sprayer. It's now pointed at my face. I quickly flip him back on his belly. But, he begins squirming. It's getting hard to hold him.

My course of action becomes clear. Get him over the fence and into the tall grass **immediately**. I speed walk with Sadie at my heels, plow into the tall grass, and head for a stretch of good east fence. He's squirming more now, I'm afraid I'll drop him and Sadie will be there to recover him.

I keep my hands cupped together, reach the four-foot high wire fence, lean as far over the barbed-wire top as I can and gently release him into the protective custody of the tall grass.

Sadie tries to go after him but the fence intervenes. "Com'on girl. It's time to go." I look over the fence one last time. He isn't moving. Maybe I should have kept him.

We walk back to the pen and I pet the girls as they eat their breakfast. I keep my distance from Abbey's face. I don't care much for her *eau de skunk* perfume.

After the girls eat, I walk back to the place where I had released the little guy. He still hasn't moved. I go to work and worry all day if I did the right thing.

I get home from work and go to the place where he'd been 10 hours earlier. To my relief, he's nowhere to be seen. Found by his parents, I hope, and led back home to safety.

I wonder what he'll tell them about his adventure this morning? Years from now, I wonder if he'll even remember his encounter with a human being. I know I'll never forget my encounter with him…

…that little stinker.

CHAPTER THREE

LIVING LIFE

No farmer ever plowed a field by turning it over in his mind.

—Anonymous

Are you cut out for country life?

"Green Acres is the place to be.
Farm livin' is the life for me.
Land spreadin' out so far and wide.
Keep Manhattan just give me that countryside…"

The theme song from the classic TV show "Green Acres" pretty much says it all. While others choose to live in the city or in the suburbs close to their neighbors, we like a place with a little more space.

In our neighborhood, most houses are built on a minimum of 10-acre parcels. There are a few exceptions, of course. Our neighbors to the west sit on five acres and our neighbors to the east own 30. And, we have seven — the acreage remaining with the original farmhouse after a previous owner split this land. But, whether we have seven or 70 acres, the farm will always be our oasis – our haven in a hectic world.

It starts with the crisp, full-bodied country morning air. The aroma of baled hay mixes with a waft of fallen leaves and (depending on the prevailing winds) either a whiff of manure or a hint of *eau de skunk* to produce a fresh, bold scent that's pleasant enough to us country folks (but would probably never be a hit at the perfume counter).

The country sky is filled with blackbirds cawing, ducks quacking and geese honking as they fly in formation looking for their next meal or watering hole. Neighboring horses nicker in their stalls, while sheep graze silently in the morning fog as barnyard dogs discourage possible trespassers.

The fresh air and country sounds are only part of what we cherish about our country life. We also love the freedom to use our land in whatever way we choose: to raise livestock, plant crops, add a barn (Charley's favorite) or leave it natural. And, when we want to get away from it all, we only have to walk out our back door to commune with nature's beauty.

But not far from our backyard the countryside is changing. More and more open spaces are steadily, quietly being transformed into pockets of suburbia. Developers from the city are discovering our oasis, buying up large parcels, getting them rezoned to accommodate small lots, building big homes on those small lots and selling them to people who might not appreciate what it's like to live in the country.

Recently we learned of such a proposed development not half a mile from our front door. We, along with a large number of our neighbors, appeared at the township planning and zoning board to speak in favor of retaining the 10-acre zoning currently assigned to the 160-acre parcel.

The developers were asking to put 102 homes on the site rather than the 16 homes allowed for by the current zoning. We explained to the commissioners, we don't begrudge developers their freedom to buy the land and develop it. We just want to preserve a bit of the country for those who want some land around them.

The commissioners heard quite a bit of testimony that night, taking it all under advisement. Then two weeks later, they denied the developer's request to rezone the parcel. We were ecstatic until we found out that the commissioner's decision is actually a recommendation that gets passed along to the township council for final decision. That vote comes up next week. You can be sure we'll be there.

In the meantime, I've just read about another 170-home development that's being built on 288 acres about a mile from us. That rezoning has already been approved and eventually we'll have 170 new neighbors, many without country-living experience.

Since we can't stop developments, maybe we can at least recruit people to the area who will understand and respect our country way of life. I propose that we help prospective buyers decide if they're cut out for country living by having them complete the following checklist.

Instructions: Please check all that apply.
You know you can survive in the country, if you...
__like the smell of manure.
__understand why there's a market for bat-proof mailboxes.
__can get along without paved roads, sidewalks, and streetlights.
__never rake your leaves.
__don't lose sleep over crab grass.
__know that cow pies are not a type of dessert.
__have ever hauled something in a pick-up truck.
__can operate a riding lawn mower.
__acknowledge passers-by with a friendly nod or wave.
__know the difference between pets and livestock.
__own or dream of owning a generator.
__know the difference between hay and straw.
__have ever seen a live opossum.
__have ever worn overalls to do chores.
__enjoy the taste of real water from a well – not that treated city stuff.

__know where the contents of a country toilet go when it's flushed.

__realize that eventually someone will have to pump out that stuff from your country toilet and haul it away.

__look natural in baseball caps advertising feed, fertilizer or farm implements.

__are patient when driving behind a farm tractor going 10 miles an hour on a two-lane road in a no-passing zone.

__love and respect the land and all the creatures that depend on it.

Score: 100% (20 checks)
Welcome to country life!

Score: 95% (19 checks or less)
You might want to think twice about country living. But don't worry, there are hundreds of existing, great homes in the suburbs that will suit your lifestyle, complete with mature trees, city water, city sewer, fenced-in yard, and plenty of neighbors close by.

Plus, you won't have to breathe in any of that full-bodied country-morning air…

Helpful household hints

I grew up in a suburb of Detroit with cookie-cutter houses and postage-stamp size yards. The streets were paved and so were the sidewalks. It was a "Donna Reed" world where moms stayed home and dads went to work.

Thanks to my mom, our house ran with precision. Everything was neat, clean and on schedule. The cereal boxes, bowls and juice glasses were set out each evening before bed so they would be ready for breakfast the next day. Lunches were packed in the morning so they'd be fresh and were handed to us as we ran out the door for the school bus. We ate dinner every weeknight at 5:30 when dad got home.

Mondays were wash days and clothes were hung outside on the line to dry in the sun and fresh air. **Tuesdays** the ironing got done — including underwear and sheets "because they fit better in the drawers." (I can still iron a mean pair of boxer shorts but there's not much call for that anymore.)

On **weekdays** when there was a good breeze and low humidity "it was a good day to wash floors." And, she did. Why, they were so clean my dad would often say, "we could eat off these floors." In the evenings, she would darn socks, sew on buttons, or fashion a new outfit for one of us on the sewing machine. **Saturdays** were reserved for grocery shopping and errands. **Sundays** meant church and family.

There were also seasonal undertakings — like spring cleaning. Every year at the first hint of spring, mom and dad would take down all the storm windows, put them in storage and put up the screens. Before installing the screens, mom would carefully wash the inside and outside of each window, removing the grime from the long winter, allowing the glorious sunshine to stream in streak-free.

It was during this time of spring cleaning that she would do extra little things. I remember her taking a nut pick, covering it with a wash cloth and carefully tracing every small opening in every heat register in the house to make sure each was clean and fresh for the new season.

This, of course, was in addition to washing walls, cleaning light fixtures, using a toothbrush to clean the grout in between the ceramic tile on the kitchen counter and bathroom walls and bringing up the spring clothes from the cedar closet and swapping them for our winter duds.

She was very serious about taking care of her family and our home. **It was her full-time job and she was always on duty — especially with five kids.** We didn't have fancy furnishings but the house always looked neat, clean and company-ready. That's the way I was taught. That was my example. And, that's the standard I've tried to use.

There's just one problem. **It doesn't work!** Although my first allegiance is to my family and home, my attention and energy are divided among family, pets, full-time job, part-time writing, outside groups, recreational activities, and housekeeping. And, it's pretty much in that that order. Needless to say, when it comes to housekeeping, I usually have very little attention or energy left.

That's why our house operates on a modified version of my mother's routine. We still run errands on Saturdays. Sundays are still reserved for church. But, the rest of Donna

Reed's world is gone and Martha Stewart (obviously) doesn't have our schedule. Here's what works for us.

Wash day can be any day that we are about to run out of clean underwear and preferably before one of us actually does. If the weather is nice, time permits, and the dogs are in their pen, clothes are hung outside on the line. But usually they're thrown in the dryer and pesky line-dry items are draped strategically around the house to air dry.

Ironing is done as a last resort. Permanent press shirts are hung up, hopefully, still warm from the dryer. Underwear may be folded and placed neatly in drawers. On those crazy days, it's acceptable to leave clean unmentionables in the laundry basket and make your selections from there.

Mending consists of buttons that are sewn on by hand, either in an emergency or when the last one on a garment has finally fallen off. Socks with gaping holes are relegated to the rag bag and the sewing machine is rarely used since its cabinet doubles as a television stand.

Floors get washed when feet actually stick to them. Note: Spot cleaning of sticky areas is acceptable when time is limited. When a complete wash is possible but it's not "a good day to wash floors," a fan can be used to create dry, breezy conditions.

Dinner is served in the evening between 5:30 and 10:30 and can be eaten in shifts. It is often planned on the drive home from work. Anything easy, quick, thawed-out or microwavable will do. Calls can also be made from your car phone to order pizza, as long as you can pick it up on your way home. Consider ordering a Greek or tossed salad to give your family the greens they need.

Lunches are packed the night before — providing the packer can stay awake — and include a breakfast bar that can be eaten on the drive to work. Coffee, juice, and vitamins are swallowed on the way out the door in the morning.

Grocery shopping gets done when there's no more milk, usually after work on an evening when there isn't a meeting. Coupons are left on the kitchen counter waiting to be clipped and returnables are forgotten in the garage.

Spring cleaning can be done anytime of the year. When large blocks of time are unavailable, concentrate on those noticeable items like cobwebs and dust bunnies and high traffic areas like your entry way, kitchen and bathroom. If all else fails, consider using candlelight. Then no one can tell if you've actually washed your walls, cleaned the light fixtures or dusted.

Dusting is optional, especially if you live on a dirt road that's muddy in the spring and dusty in the summer and all of this dirt seems to make its way into your 110-year-old farm house. In this case, make a rule that it's okay to write in the dust on various surfaces, as long as you don't include the date.

If you follow these simple tips, your family's basic needs will be met and the inside of your home will always be company-ready — providing the company who plans to "drop by," calls first and gives you ample time to pick up the wash you've draped all over the house.

And, as for cleaning those storm windows, I think I've got that figured out, too....

"Hey, Charley, fire up that new power washer!"

It's about time...

It's spring and I'm suffering from a malady that strikes about this time every year. Maybe you've got it, too. I call it Daylight Saving Time Lag. It hits the day we set our clocks ahead one hour and lasts anywhere from a few days to a few weeks while my body get used to the time change. This year, the "Lag" has hit me especially hard.

I know *why* we make the change and I sure enjoy the extra hour of daylight we get on a warm summer's evening. I don't even mind falling back. It's just that this "springing forward" thing deprives me of sleep. And, the older I get the less "springy" I am. When we first make the change, I certainly am not springing out of bed in the morning as my nightstand clock announces it's 5:15, because my body clock is painfully aware that it's really only 4:15!

And, what about the animals? They're governed by their internal clocks, too (in spite of the goofy rooster across the street who crows at all hours). So when I arrive an hour early for their morning walk, even the dogs are groggy.

Come to think of it, when Daylight Saving Time was first conceived, did anyone ask the livestock what they thought of the idea? I guess by now cows would say it's a *moot* point.

Speaking of having a say, did we ever vote on Daylight Saving Time? Did we ever actually agree to this falling back and springing forward thing? Do we *have* to comply?

They don't observe it in Arizona, you know. My sister lives there and Arizonans just decided not to participate. So, in the summertime they're three hours behind us and in the winter, they're two hours behind. And, *they* don't seem any worse for the wear.

The Daylight Saving Time concept makes sense — to give us more daylight so we can get more things done. But, the application needs a little work. And, I've been too busy changing

> alarm clocks, wall clocks, bathroom clocks,
> mud room clocks, VCR clocks, microwave clocks,
> breadmaker clocks, computer clocks, electronic
> thermostat clocks, answering machine clocks,
> watches, car clocks (difficult but not impossible
> to do while driving), truck clocks, barn clocks, and
> garage clocks

to give it much thought.

I do know time is a precious commodity. I try to *save it* all the time. When I'm driving to work, along with hundreds of other motorists, I try to *make up for lost time*. That's because I've *wasted time* somewhere else along the way. But my real goal in life is to *spend my time* doing what I like to do (and find someone who will pay me to do it!).

I know I'm not the only person preoccupied with time. Surely on more than one occasion, you've heard that:

> Time is money.
> Time heals all wounds.
> Time is of the essence.
> A stitch in time, saves nine.
> No time like the present.

If you don't have the time to do it right, will you
  have the time to do it over?
Everyone is given the same 24 hours in a day.
The older you get the faster time goes.
Time flies when you're having fun.
This is the last time I'm going to tell you.
The third time is the charm.
Time waits for no one.
If you can manage time, you can manage your life.

OK, so if all of this is true, wouldn't it help everyone if we had a few more hours in the day? If the government can legislate *time changes*, why can't they *add time*?

That's it! Now there's something I'd vote for—adding two extra hours to each Daylight Saving Time Day. But, there'd have to be a few restrictions on how those hours could be used. The first priority would be to use them for extra sleep or extra fun. It would be forbidden to use them for extra work!

We could call it "Daylight Saving Elastic Time." Then in the spring we could "spring and stretch forward" and in the winter we could "fall and shrink back." I *know* we could sell this idea. Write your senator! Call your congressperson! Talk with your favorite cow! She'd probably advise you to *moove* ahead with it.

And, until we're able to make it the law of the land, I'll fly to my sister's in Arizona and gain a few more hours for at least for one day. Just think of all the extra things I can get done...or maybe I'll just get caught up on my sleep!

Batteries not required

As I sat in the gym watching the boy's varsity basketball game, Ashley, a petite third grader, tugged on my skirt. "Can you get my dog unstuck?" she asked. As I looked around, wondering why a four-legged mutt would be in the gym, she handed me a palm-sized, square object with a screen. It was her virtual pet dog. He was frozen in place and no matter what button she pushed he refused to budge, or bark, or beg, ... or whatever it was that he was supposed to do.

I didn't have the heart to tell her I had no experience in treating such "animals," so I pushed all the buttons — nothing. Then I turned the "dog" over on its back. The directions said to push the restart button to revive the pet. As I looked for the button, I said with authority, "Ah yes, we just need to press the restart button. Do you know where it is?"

"No," she replied. "It broke off last week." "Oh," I said. "Well, then try replacing the battery." Sensing that I'd reached my level of technical incompetence and wanting to let me down gently, she plucked her "pet" out of my hand, slipped it into her back pocket and skipped away saying, "That's OK. I'll just ask my mom to buy me another one."

Then, the other day at work, my secretary, Janet, was trying to find a map to her nephew's house. Her out-of-town sister was going to be there visiting and Janet wanted to see her. So, she was trying to use the handy feature on the Internet that draws a map after you've given the address, cross roads, city, state, zip code and country of your desired destination.

Alas, Janet had received incomplete information from her sister, so the results were wrong. And, after involving several other people in problem solving, she still had no map. Just when she and two other co-workers were staring blank-faced at her computer screen, a third co-worker happened by, pulled out an old-fashioned paper road map and gave her the information she needed.

Or, how about the caller on the local radio station who was lamenting about not being able to get on a web site to download a software program? She needed the software to get her IRS forms via the Internet. She had tried several different times of the day and was never able to get on the system.

The radio host suggested she try dialing in very early in the morning to avoid competing with calls from the West coast. She said she'd tried that and it hadn't worked either. She finally gave up and called the IRS on the telephone and asked them to mail her the forms.

And, then there was the cheering father of a sixth grade player from the opposing side. "It's great that your son came out for the team. Do you practice a lot at home?" I asked, trying to make polite conversation.

"No," the frustrated father answered. "When I was a kid, no one needed to encourage us to go outside and play ball. We found a bushel basket, set it up in the alley, and had ourselves a pick-up game. But, today it's hard to get my son outside to play...what with the computer, television, and video games."

Now all this makes me wonder...is the technology that's making our lives easier, also causing techno-trouble? Is the lure of convenience and the promise of saved time, lulling us into mindless technology dependence?

Time for a reality check. How many of the things you've used today relied on some kind of technology? And, how many of those really saved you time or were better than the "old fashioned" way?

Well, living on the farm, I'm pleased to say, that while I do rely on a **few** modern conveniences, I certainly don't consider myself to be **techno-dependent**.

Take this morning. I woke up in a thermostatically-controlled heated house after hitting the snooze several times on my electric alarm clock, got milk and juice out of the frig, made oatmeal in the microwave, made coffee in the coffee maker, took a shower with water pumped up from our well, listened to the radio for weather, dressed in clothes that were washed and dried in machines and am now writing this piece using a computer to record my words, a spell checker to verify their accuracy, a desk lamp to illuminate them, and a printer to get them from a monitor screen onto paper.

OK. So, everything I've used this morning has had some kind of technology boost. We may live in a farmhouse that was built in the 19th century, but we're entitled to have 21st century technology. It's not like it's against the law or anything. And, it's not like I can't do without technology.

Yeah, that's it. Why I'm sure I can find lots of low-tech replacements for the high-tech gizmos we use around here...

High Tech	Low Tech
desk lamp	candle
television news	newspaper
videotaped movie	book
vacuum cleaner	broom and dust pan
brewed coffee	sun tea

weather channel	outside thermometer/window
video game	board game
digital clock	wind-up clock
computer	paper and pencil
printer	manual typewriter
e-mail message	postcard
phone call	stop by to visit
tread mill	walk outside
electric fan	southern breeze
clothes dryer	clothesline
credit card	cash
~~dishwasher~~	~~sink and dish soap~~
~~electric drill~~	~~hand drill~~

Charley crossed out the electric drill entry because he says there are just some technological improvements that are critical to human survival. I agree. (That's why I crossed out the dishwasher!)

And, even more importantly, there are some low-tech items that are absolutely essential to our very existence, like kindness, hugs and quality time with loved ones.

The key is to find a balance between the two. So, right after I print this out on my high-tech printer, I'm meeting Charley outside for a low-tech walk with our real dogs.

You remember real dogs, don't you? They don't need reset buttons. They only need to see our faces and hear our voices to have their batteries recharged!

The clothes make the man

Charley's idea of getting dressed up to go out is putting on his jeans, a shirt with a collar, his cowboy boots and topping it off with his canvass field coat.

So, last week when he announced, "I might need a new suit." I wondered aloud, "what's the occasion?" because given a choice between shopping and a root canal, Charley would, without hesitation, beat a path to the dentist.

"John's getting married," Charley announced, "and the suit I got for Brad's graduation is starting to show its age."

Starting to show its age? Brad graduated from high school 12 years ago. And, although it was a quality suit at the time, 12 years is a lot to ask of any piece of fabric.

"Well, dear, it's up to you," I said, secretly pleased. "But, if we're going suit shopping, we need to do it soon to allow enough time for any alterations. "

"Okay," he said, "let's go next Saturday."

Saturday a storm dumped eight inches of snow on us. "Can't go shopping today," Charley announced with relief in his voice. "The roads are terrible and the mall parking lots will be a mess."

"How about tomorrow after church?" I asked, not letting him off the hook. "We'll see," he said.

Sunday morning came and I saw my opportunity. "The sun is out. Roads are dry. And, we're already in our good clothes. If we grab a quick bite after church and head to the mall, it shouldn't take us long." (The pep talk was as much for me as for Charley since my shopping usually involves a catalog and a phone.) "All right," he said, "we'll go after lunch."

We downed our sandwiches, Charley grabbed his cowboy boots and we took off. As we motored toward the mall, we discussed whether we should go to the department store or the specialty shop that sells "suits and more." We opted for the specialty store.

A salesman, with a tape measure hanging around his neck and an outstretched hand, greeted us at the door. "Hi, my name is Ron. What are you folks looking for today?" "Hi Ron, I'm Gerri and this is my husband, Charley. He needs a suit."

Ron's eyes sparkled as he sprang into action. "Okay, Charley, come right over here." As we walked, Ron began figuring aloud what size Charley might wear.

"Let's see. You look like a regular." We stopped in front of the regular suits and Ron whipped his tape measure from around his neck, first encircling Charley's chest, then his waist, noting the measurements while never missing a beat in his monologue.

"I see you wear boots. You wear them with your suits? Great. That way we can be sure to get the pants hemmed to the right length."

By now he was reaching into the rack and pulling out suit coats. "Try this on for size." Charley complied as the patter continued.

"What colors do you like? You're fair skinned, this is a great shade of olive green." He could tell by Charley's expression that green wasn't getting it. "I bet you're more of a blue man."

Ron handed Charley a suit coat that was similar in style and color to his old suit at home. But it was a little big. "You're in-between sizes. We can take up the sleeves and move the button over, if you want this color.

"Or, better yet, try this one," Ron said, handing Charley a medium-gray jacket with a blue windowpane pattern running through it. "It's a popular, American-made brand. We just got this style in. I really like it. And it fits you well. Now, of course, you'll be wearing suit pants instead of those bulky casual pants and that will make a difference. What do you think?" As I eyed the fit, Ron continued.

"Now let's talk pants. Have you ever worn suspenders, Charley? I don't know about you, but I've put on 30 pounds over the last year and my whole attitude about suspenders has changed. You can wear your pants a little looser, so you don't have to unbutton that top button after you push yourself away from the table, and your pants won't fall down around your knees.

"Suspenders are definitely the way to go. They're in and the pants that go with that gray suit jacket have the suspender buttons built in. You'll look great. You're long waisted. We've got tall suspenders over here. I'll just get you some."

Ron was gone and back in an instant, still talking. "Charley, let's get you into a fitting room and see how these pants and suspenders look with the jacket."

After our new found friend, Ron, whisked Charley away, he came back with three different shirts and three different ties holding them up against the gray and blue windowpane jacket. "Well, Ger, what do you think? I like this French blue shirt with this tie. It brightens up the suit."

I hadn't planned on buying a shirt and tie. Charley has plenty of both at home. Besides, I wondered, how much do they want for a shirt and tie here?

"It's refreshing to see a couple like you and Charley, you get along so well. Some people come in here and they're grouchy, snapping at each other…Now me, I'm 39 and never been married, never found the right woman, that is until now. That's her over there."

I listened as my buddy Ron confided in me about his co-worker who also happened to be his significant other. He's really a congenial guy, I thought, and proceeded to choose the light gray shirt and royal blue and gray patterned tie.

Just as I started thinking about prices again, Charley appeared with the suit pants on and a lot of extra material puddled around his ankles. "Hey, they look great," Ron offered. "Oh, don't worry about that extra fullness," Ron said in response to Charley's tugging at the unfamiliar pleats in front. "It's the style, besides we're going to take 'em in at the back. You're like me in that department, Charley; you don't have much in the seat…

"We'll have you fixed up in a minute. I'll just get Jimmy, our tailor, over here. Hey, Jimmy…"

Before we could blink, Jimmy appeared with chalk in hand, marking where the excess fabric would be taken in or cut off. Charley stood looking tentatively at his reflection in the three-way mirror. But Ron was there to reassure him. "You're gonna look like a million bucks…"

Once Jimmy finished, there wasn't much more to do. Charley retreated to the fitting room, changed back into his comfortable clothes and brought the suit out to Ron.

"Would you like some socks to go with that?" Ron asked. "No thanks," Charley said. "If I'm wearing my boots, I can wear my softball socks and no one will know!" We laughed. Charley was finished shopping.

Ron backed off and entered the price tag information into the computer. With a $25 fee for alterations it came to a three-figure amount that took us by surprise. But helpful Ron was there once again. "I know it looks like a lot, but if you take that amount and divide it by the number of years you're going to wear this suit—it's a bargain. Besides, if you ever need the seams let out that have been taken in, we'll do it for free and we offer free pressing."

We left the store figuring that Charley will have to wear the suit for twenty years before the per year amount will be what it would have been if we'd bought a suit from the department store.

But it was worth it to see Ron, the super salesman, in action. He did know his business and he did get us in and out of there in 90 minutes. You have to admire a professional like that. Besides, Ron asked Jimmy to put a rush on the alterations for us. You can't get that combination of service and entertainment just anywhere.

Now let's see, Charley should be all set for John's wedding: suit, shirt, tie, suspenders, boots, baseball socks. Oops, he doesn't have a dress overcoat. Not to worry. I'm sure Ron will be happy to sell us one when we pick up Charley's altered suit next weekend.

On second thought, Charley's canvass field coat is looking mighty good right about now.

Do you copy?

Recently, I've discovered a "not-so-new" radio station and now every morning when I get into my car, I can't wait to tune it in. This frequency specializes in broadcasting local traffic conditions (a must for us road warriors), and it also has weather, jokes, human interest stories, advice, and the occasional cut of music.

But, mostly it's 24 hours a day of uncensored, adult talk-radio where the callers are the "on-air personalities." They talk to their "good buddies" always asking if they've got their "ears on" (I never leave the house without mine) and seem to be very concerned about bears. In particular, they're always on the look out for that Smokey Bear and will often tell where he's hiding so others can see him, too (how thoughtful).

I haven't called-in to the station because the "callers" speak a kind of language that I've yet to master. And, the radio equipment seems to be fragile. I can't tell you how many times I've heard someone call-in and say, "Break one-nine for a radio check." I guess calling-in is hard on the equipment, so I'll be satisfied to just listen for a while longer.

As I listen, I'm learning a lot about the "callers," their wisdom, wit and world. Most of them drive 18-wheelers, making their living on the road. They answer to handles like Cowboy and Wild Man (with an occasional Super Woman thrown in) and I have a new appreciation for them. Everyday they give me valuable information, warn me of possible danger, remind me to drive safely and make me smile.

Here's some of the jaw jacking I've been hearing lately.

Highway advice:

In this exchange, one driver is complaining to another about a four-wheeler he just can't shake. "When I speed up to 65, he goes 65. When I slow down to 55, he goes 55."

The second driver suggests to the first, "**Why don't you stop** and see what he does."

Weather reports:

In a blizzard on a two-lane in morning rush hour, one driver asks, "How 'bout cha, northbound. What's the weather report?"

Quickly comes the reply. "It's snowing."

Local information:

A driver trying to find a fuel stop asks: "Where's the nearest northbound truck stop?"

A good buddy answers: "At that 67, driver. The fuel sells for 131."

"I'd rather put water in this old rig than spend that much money," says driver one.

"Maybe if you put water in it, you'd get a new rig," observes the second driver.

Number one comes back: "That's a big 10-4 and I'd have to get a new job, too."

Some messages are more serious.

Road safety:

Several hours after sunset on a snow-covered road, one driver reports, "Just after the 145 on the westbound side, looks like there's a four-wheeler in the ditch and they're going to try to push it out by hand. Be careful."

Driving etiquette:
    In a recent snow storm on that northbound side during the evening rush hour, two good buddies are wishing that all of us four-wheelers would speed up or stay in the right lane, so they can have the open space ahead.
    "Do these four-wheelers need a lesson to remind them that slower traffic is supposed to stay to the right? If this guy in front of me puts on his brakes, I'll have nowhere to go. I'll have to hit him," says driver one.
    "I guess they forget that they can stop a heck of a lot easier than us loaded 18-wheelers can!" suggests driver number two.
    That's all the lesson I need. I move over to the right lane and stay there.

    Like I said, all this information has been valuable — even entertaining. And, I think I'm beginning to pick up some of the lingo.

    Oh wait a second, I hear a good buddy on my radio now. He's giving a traffic report for the highway that I'm traveling — which is always congested especially at rush hour. Here he is:
    "Well, northbound, it looks to me like what you've got is too many cars and not enough road."
    Amen! You hit the nail on the head. I mean — 10-4 good buddy. That's a Roger. I copy that. I'm gonna put the hammer down and be your front door, so we can put that Tree City in our back pocket and head for home. I've heard tell it's clean and green most of the way to that Buick City. But we've gotta be careful 'cuz there's a bear at 53 in the middle

in the dark and those bridges are gettin' kinda greasy 'cuz of the snow. So, big truck, com'on over and we'll have ourselves a convoy before we get stuck in that parking lot and have to go way below that double nickel. What's that driver? I'm losin' you. Have a safe trip, driver. Catch you on the flip flop. And, next time you're out this way, ask if that Funny Farm Gal has her ears on...

Note: There are more than 30 million Citizen Band (CB) radios in operation in the United States and several million more in operation in Canada, Jamaica and Germany. Each radio has 40 channels. Channel 9 is reserved for emergency communication and Channel 19 is widely used by truckers and motorists. The other 38 channels are for general use.

Thanks for the memories

We've been together for more than eight years and now it's come to an end. I'm devastated. I'm inconsolable. I'm miserable. I'm in denial. The bond we had developed over these last several, wonderful years had nourished me. It provided me with almost everything I required to survive. Whenever I needed the least little thing, I knew I could turn to you. Now, what will I do? Now where will I go?

I don't understand how eight years of loyalty, trust and faithfulness can just be cast aside in an instant. I never saw it coming. I hadn't a clue that things weren't working out. Over the years I had shared my innermost hungers. Because of what I had received from you, I was able to give to others, reaching out to them in times of celebration and sorrow.

Don't get me wrong. On some days I paid a high price for hanging in there. But I felt it was worth every penny. None other could compare.

My friend, Pat, who had been through a similar situation not too long ago, reminded me that I was less than sympathetic in her time of need. I apologized. How could I have been so unfeeling? Accepting my apology, graciously she offered to go with me to pick up the last few items that remained. "No one should have to do this alone," Pat said trying to comfort me.

As we drove into the driveway, there it was for all to see. There was no denying it now. The sign read, "All items 33% off—Food Town Going out of Business Sale." It had come to this, I had bought your groceries and produce for nearly a decade, spending most of my Friday nights among your aisles and this is the thanks I get?

And, what about last spring when you reorganized the store and I couldn't find anything? Did I leave? Did I slink around and shop at a competitor? No. I hung in there. I'm even proud to say I was finally beginning to find all my favorite products again and now it's gone, all gone.

Now where will I go? There's no other grocery store on my way home from work. Grocery shopping is not exactly something I love to do. And, now it's become that much harder.

Oh, I don't blame the store managers or the employees. I know that you shopped here, too. It's that national chain that bought out your lease. Do they think I'm going to travel 13 miles out of my way to shop at their store in the next town? And, even if they're planning to build a new store somewhere close by, do they think I'll forget the inconvenience they've put me through?

DON'T MESS WITH MY NEIGHBORHOOD GROCERY STORE!! Because you see, it's more than where I stop to get food. It's a place I can depend on to be there for me morning and night—when I'm out of milk or need that special ingredient for the recipe I'm in the middle of making.

It's a place to see people from the neighborhood and from church. It's where I buy my birthday cards, wedding cards, anniversary cards and sympathy cards. It's where I buy our Halloween and Easter candy, the holiday turkeys, the special desserts, and the deli salads for family picnics (that so conveniently slip from your containers into mine, leading others to believe they're homemade). It's where I buy pop to soothe upset stomachs, aspirin to ease pain, and vitamins to bolster our immune systems.

It's where I stop and chat with my favorite stock boy whose paychecks have given him spending money all through high school and are now helping him pay for college. It's where I see the familiar faces of the cashiers and the baggers and enjoy their friendly banter.

It's where I recycle my plastic bags, take back hundreds (maybe thousands) of dollars worth of cans and bottles, exchange clipped coupons for the face value amount and double on Sundays. It's where you always let me write my checks for $20 over the total amount so I have mad money for the upcoming week.

It's where I've tried new culinary delights like fancy marinades, pastas, beans, soups, and produce. And, it's where I've learned that there are some culinary delights that I won't try again. It's where I discovered the joys of lite ice cream, reduced fat sour cream, and turkey bologna (don't tell Charley—he still thinks he's eating the fat-laden stuff).

It's been a nourishing relationship in so many ways. It's hard to let go.

As I wheel my cart down the nearly bare aisles, I note that even store furnishings are for sale. The end is really here. Pat wheels her cart next to mine and says, "I have to go. Are you going to be okay here, alone." "Sure," I said, "You go on. I just need to get a few more things."

Soon we'll have digested all of the evidence of this great relationship. I think to myself, *I need to find something more lasting.* As I turn down the next aisle, I spy well-worn wooden crates for sale: two for $5. An employee tells me they were used for many years to unload produce. "A keepsake!" I say to myself as I put one in my cart. In Aisle 4, I find a set of corn-on-the-cob skewers, in Aisle 5 a woven basket—more memorabilia.

In the last aisle, I stop and chat with the manager and he tells me all the employees will be placed at other stores. It makes me feel a little better. I go through the checkout line, thank the cashier for her years of service, and ask where she'll go. She starts at the store in the neighboring town on Monday. "Good luck," I say. "Maybe I'll see you there sometime."

I arrive home, unload the Food Town grocery bags for the last time, fold them neatly and put them away. "I'll feel better in the morning," I say to myself....

...In the morning as Charley poured the last of the milk on his cereal, I said, "That was the last of the Food Town milk. I saved it for you." He looked at me, decided not to crack a smile, and replied as seriously as he could, "Thank you. I'll savor it."

And, I'll savor my eight years of fond grocery-shopping memories. Thanks, Food Town!

Note: Family-owned Food Town served the Hartland area for more than 25 years.

The reluctant reunion

This is your second notice! Don't miss it. Send in your money by the deadline to make sure there's a seat for you.

Well, it may have been the second notice, but it was the first I had heard about it.

Did I really want to spend a Saturday evening with a bunch of people I might have known all those years ago?

As I debated, Charley said, "It's up to you. I'll go if you do. But, I'm certainly not going without you!"

Charley has never missed one of his class reunions. Coming from a small town high school with a graduating class of 42 and him being the class president and all...I think he'd be missed.

As for me, there were 800 seniors in my suburban high school of 2,400. Who'd miss me?

Besides, most of the people on the list of those "not found" were kids I hung around with. Would I even know anyone if I went?

"I'll think about it," I said and put the invitation in the "to do something with pile." For the next few weeks, I hoped for another engagement to conflict...a wedding, a dinner invitation, elective surgery, an emergency trip to the grocery store.... Nothing.

With no good excuse, a willing escort, and the deadline at hand, I felt guilty and sent in my money.

The evening of the reunion came. We dressed, told Charley's son, Brad, we'd be home early and left.

As we drove to the banquet hall, Charley made conversation. "So, what did you do in high school?"

That was a good question. High school seemed so long ago. Let's see...I didn't do cheerleading or extra curricular activities. I didn't do student council. I wasn't involved in sports. I'm sure it was because there weren't many opportunities for girls in sports back then. (It couldn't have been because I was so uncoordinated.) Let's see...what did I do in school? Oh, yeah.

"I was involved in choir," I announced, pleased to have found something to show I'd done more than just take up time and space.

You see, when I was in high school, I didn't have time for extra-curricular stuff because I had more important things to do. I had a part-time position as a candy-counter girl at the local movie theatre. The kids who worked there were from several local high schools, and we soon formed our own circle of friends. Hmmm. Maybe I'd see some of them at the reunion.

As we pulled into the banquet hall parking lot, my reluctance gave way to curiosity. (I think that was Charley's plan, all along.)

I wondered aloud who'd be there and how they'd look. Charley (always sensible) suggested we "go in and see."

We found the registration desk and got our nametags. Mine featured the usual cheesy photocopied yearbook picture. *How **did** I get my hair to stay in that flip?*

As we entered the dimly lit room, all I could see were a lot of grown-up strangers in fancy clothes. As my eyes adjusted, some familiar faces emerged from the crowd: a fellow former candy-counter girl, two neighbor girls, then a third girl from the old neighborhood. Seeing these friendly faces, I was drawn into the crowd and hugs and conversation came naturally.

"How've you been? What are you doing now? How is your family? Are your folks still around?" I left Charley to fend for himself as I got caught up with my classmates.

Soon we were summoned to take the class photo. It took a while for us to gather under the photographer's bright lights (revealing some of life's inevitable changes like wrinkles, gray hair or less hair). Even so, for a brief moment we acted like high schoolers again, resisting the photographer as he tried to pose us.

Most ignored his instructions. Many were involved in side conversations. A few were clowning around. Some refused to sit on the floor in front or to move closer together. In the end, the photographer — resigned to our minimal cooperation — backed up his ladder until he could see all of us in his view finder and snapped the picture. (The bad news is, we'll be a bunch of pin heads. The good news is, you won't be able to see our wrinkles.)

After the photo session, we ate dinner. We sat with Chris and Roger. They had been great friends in high school but married other people. A few years ago, Chris divorced and Roger's wife passed away. Then, Roger called Chris' mom to see how Chris was doing and now they're engaged and planning to move back to the old neighborhood.

Come to think of it, they were one of the few couples who were there. I was amazed at how many of my classmates came without their spouses — unless of course, their spouse had also been a classmate like the homecoming queen's husband or the star football player and his cheerleader wife.

That makes it even more special that Charley came with me. (And, that's why it's important for me to make sure he isn't bored.) Oh, here comes Barb from my old neighborhood.

She now lives in Missouri close to where Charley grew up. "Hi Barb. How are you?" I asked. "Great," she said. "Now, if you'll excuse me, I need to talk with Charley." And off they went, leaving me to wonder just whose class reunion this was?

So, I ventured off on my own to discover who the guy was that no one recognized, to learn about a classmate who lost his shirt in the Texas oil drought, to hear about a friend who passed away, to empathize with the classmate who owns a small business and can't find good employees, to learn about the profitability of worm farming from an entrepreneur and to dance to tunes spun by a 22-year-old DJ who had never played for a class reunion before and, had yet to attend his own class reunion!

We finally heard some music from our era when members of the old high school garage band — who hadn't been together in 20 years — played some selections including a decent rendition of In A Godda Da Vida.

During the band's set, I managed to find Kim, a kid from my grammar school class. For eight years, he'd sat in front of me, since my last name followed his in the alphabet and all our teachers preferred alphabetical seating. (I think one year they got creative and did reverse alphabetical order to give us the back of someone else's head to look at.) Anyway....

We talked about the good old days in grammar school. And how, if we needed any construction work done, he was the one to call.

Before I knew it, our baby DJ was announcing the last song and the evening was coming to a close. As Charley and I said our good-byes and made our way to the door, Kim stopped me and said, "You know, we really should get a grade school reunion together."

"That'd be great," I said. "Call me. I'd be happy to help. I **love** reunions." Charley just grinned.

Number 321?

"Number 004? Number 179? Number 424? Number 333? Number 117?…"

If the clerk calls Number 321, I'll have to go sit in that jury box and answer questions from the judge and the two attorneys to see if I'm an acceptable juror for this case.

I filled out the juror's survey two years ago. The official looking document said if I didn't, there would be legal consequences. I mailed it under protest.

For a long time I wondered if anything would come of it and then a few weeks ago I got the dreaded jury summons in the mail. I was relieved when my original summons date conflicted with an out-of-town trip.

A way out! I petitioned the court for a reprieve. They excused me. But, two weeks later I was ordered to report again, and this time there would be no excused absence.

Every day for two weeks, I was to call a toll free-number after 6 p.m. to see if my jury group was needed. I grudgingly accepted my new role as prisoner of the court system.

The first night my heart pounded as I pressed the toll-free number and listened to the instructions: "No groups are to report. Please call back Monday after 6 p.m." I was free until Monday.

Monday at 6 p.m., fighting butterflies, I punched in the 800 number and eagerly listened for what I hoped was good news. It was the same recorded voice. "No groups are to report. Please call back Tuesday after 6 p.m."

I began living day-to-day. I cleared my calendar for two weeks. Each day I left work with a clean desk, projects that were complete enough to pass along to another co-worker and voice mail messages sent to everyone who needed to know my work status. "I don't have to report for jury duty tomorrow, so I will be in the office." By the end of the first week, co-workers started chiding me, "Think they'll ever call you?"

Each night before I left the office, I "reported in" to the now familiar recorded voice relieved to hear that no groups were to report. *Maybe I wouldn't have to go.* Then on the second Monday, when I called and heard a new recorded voice my heart sank, "Groups 1-5 must report at 8:15 a.m. on Tuesday morning to the District Court building, downtown, fifth floor."

At least I knew what I'd be doing in the morning. I left voice mail messages for those who needed to know, "I won't be in the office Tuesday. I've been called for jury duty." I turned off my computer, cleared my desk, put my phone on voice mail and locked the office door.

Tuesday morning I left home at 6:50 a.m. headed for the fifth floor of a building 45 miles away. Rush hour traffic, spotty fog and orange and white construction barrels managed to eat away the extra travel time I'd allowed.

I parked my car in the designated parking structure at 8:10, still blocks away from the court. Which way now? I saw a well-dressed man emerge from a convenience store. Did he happen to know the way to district court? Yes, in fact, he was headed there. Things were looking up. My new friend, Joe the Probation Officer, walked me all the way to the fifth floor of the court building. He even directed me to the Jurors' Only area.

I thanked Joe for his kindness and entered a waiting room filled with 40 unsmiling people. I was in the right place.

At 8:25 a.m. we received our juror numbers and viewed a short video on what it means to be a juror. I found myself taking notes.

"You're what makes the system work," said the narrator. "Under Article III the US Constitution we are all entitled to a fair trial by a jury of our peers. It is up to us to make an impartial decision based on the evidence that's presented and the law.

"...You are not to talk about the case with anyone until you are instructed by the judge to deliberate. Don't talk about it with your spouse (not even Charley?). Don't listen to news accounts. Your job is to listen to the evidence in the courtroom and make an impartial decision based on what you've heard."

After the video, they called half the jurors by number and led them away to Judge Frederick's courtroom. The rest of us were called to Judge Stephens' courtroom. We rose as the judge entered the room. Before we sat down, the clerk swore us in.

Judge Stephens explained that this was a civil case. The jury would decide if the plaintiff should receive a settlement for lost wages and for pain and suffering caused by a rear-end accident. Judge Stephens instructed us not to make eye contact with or talk to either the defendant or the plaintiff. I studied both parties wondering what their life was like before and since the accident.

"...Number 054? Number 280? Number 213?"

Finally, the clerk finishes drawing the first eight numbers from the worn wooden box. Whew. Those of us whose numbers weren't called exchange glances of relief. The first eight jurors take their seats in the jury box. The judge asks if anyone has any physical disabilities that would prevent jury service? One man has a stomach ailment that he graphically describes. The judge dismisses him. The clerk calls someone to replace him. **"Number 232?"**

One is dismissed for family hardship. The clerk calls **"Number 346?"** One potential juror is an attorney who knows the defendant's attorney so he's excused. **"Number 324?"**

Gee, only three away from my number. I wonder what the courtroom looks like from the jury box?

Is there anything else the court should know that would prevent you from serving? One man objects loudly to being required to serve. The judge excuses him after checking with both attorneys.

If we all object to serving, I wonder, how can any of us have a fair trial by a jury of our peers? **"Number 259?"**

The plaintiff's attorney dismisses one because she can't say if she would be able to award damages for pain and suffering.

I think I could be open-minded and decide based on the facts. **"Number 008?"** Another is dismissed because he's been in a rear end accident that ended with a lawsuit.

It's down to six of us with one seat still open. The clerk calls **"Number 145?"** The judge asks, "If you were on trial, would you like to have someone like you on the jury?" The juror says, "Yes."

Why, of course, if I were on trial, I'd like to have someone like me on the jury. Go ahead, Madame Clerk, call juror Number 321!

Instead the judge signals to the clerk to put the numbers away and announces, "We have our jury."

The judge thanks those of us still seated in the gallery for being willing to serve. We're free to go.

Slowly I move toward the door. Lingering, I look back at the jury box and at the two parties whose fate is in the hands of a jury of their peers. A part of me wants to stay in the gallery curious to see how it turns out. The rest of me now wants to take my place in the jury box and be part of what makes the system work.

Number 321? Maybe next time.

Note: Jurors are chosen from the pool of registered voters **and also** registered drivers.

Gone fishin'

Charley plays on a Friday night softball league with his son, Brad, and a bunch of young men in their 20s and 30s. They appreciate Charley's accuracy as a pitcher and they also like him as a person. I think the camaraderie is great especially since Charley is at the tail end of his 40s.

So, when "the guys" invited Charley to go fishing with them "in a couple of weeks," he was ready. Since they were talking about going for the entire weekend (most of the guys are single), Charley (wisely) came home and checked it out with his wife before committing. (At least that's what he told me.) Could he afford the time away? "It's up to you," I said.

The next week after the Friday night ball game, Charley came home and announced, "I've decided to go fishing for one day—Saturday. David (a newlywed) doesn't want to go for the whole weekend either, so we're going to ride together and just go for the day."

"Sounds good to me," I said, imagining a quiet Saturday with the house all to myself.

That next Friday night was a softball tournament. The plan was for the guys to leave for fishing immediately after their last game (about 11:30 p.m.) and drive to the campground. Charley and David would leave at 8 the next morning to join them.

On Friday night after the game, Charley came home and said the plans had changed slightly. He was still going fishing tomorrow but David wasn't. So Charley's son, Brad, said he'd ride with him. And, they were leaving earlier than first planned so I had to get him up at 5 a.m. so he could be at Brad's by 6 a.m., so they could be at the marina in time to shove off by 8 a.m.

"No problem," I said. "I'll be happy to get you up. Just don't expect breakfast."

The next morning I woke Charley up at 5 a.m. and headed back to bed. "Bye dear, have fun." I said and never heard him leave.

The next thing I knew, the phone was ringing. I looked at the clock — it was 7 a.m. I picked up the receiver and heard Charley's irritated voice saying, "I've had it."

"Charley?" I said.

"Yeah, it's me. I'm at Brad's apartment. I've been calling him on the phone for over an hour and I haven't been able to wake him up. So, I decided to throw something against his window that would tinkle. I used my keys and now they're on the roof."

Even in my groggy state, I knew that keys probably weren't the best thing to throw at a third story window, but I decided now was not the time to mention it.

"Do you have Kristin's number?" Charley asked. "Maybe she knows where Brad is." I gave Charley her number and said, "While you call her, I'll call Brad's pager and see if I can find him." I entered the pager number and left my phone number as the automated attendant had instructed. Then I threw on some clothes and went downstairs.

The phone rang again and this time a sleepy voice, that I didn't recognize, asked, "You called me?"

"Is this Brad?" I asked. "No, this is Brian." (Brad's new roommate whom we hadn't met, yet.) "Oh, am I glad to hear from you. Charley — Brad's dad — is outside your apartment building and his keys are on your roof..."

"I'm not at the apartment," he said. "But I'll be there at 8."

"That'll work, just look for Charley in the parking lot when you get there. Thanks." I said.

I called Charley back and told him what I knew. And he told me that Kristin said Brad had gone with the guys last night and was intending to ride back with Charley (a minor miscommunication).

"Well, you'd better come over here, anyway," Charley said.

I arrived at Brad's apartment about 7:30 a.m. and found Charley staring intently at the keys laying on the roof above Brad's third floor window. "I have a plan on how to get them," he said. "We'll need to go to Meijers and get some supplies."

"But before we go, I have to see if I can reach someone at the marina and tell them I'm going to be late." The only problem was, Charley didn't know the exact name of the boat rental place or the marina. After making several more phone calls and waking up several more people, we discovered that they had gone to the Toledo Beach Marina. We left a message and drove to the store.

We bought the supplies and went back to the apartment. By now it was after 8 and there was no sign of Brad's roommate, Brian. In order to make this plan work, we had to get into the apartment and there was no one in the apartment building manager's office. I paged Brian once more and he called back. Now he was at work. We could come and get the apartment keys from him there.

Since we didn't know what he looked like, Brian told us he'd be wearing green pants and a white shirt. What he didn't tell us was that everyone who worked there would be wearing green pants and a white shirt.

We finally found Brian, got the keys and drove back to Brad's apartment. By now it was close to 9 a.m. The guys had been out on the boat for an hour and Charley was still dry-docked.

Charley never did get out on the water that day. By the time he got to the marina, the fishermen had caught their limit (about 100 walleye) and were headed back to shore.

He did get there in time to enjoy their fresh catch. They went back to the campground, ate their fill of fresh fish and baked potatoes and played a little Frisbee. Later in the evening, they sat around the campfire, and swapped fishing stories.

Even though Charley hadn't been out on the water, he had a fishing story to share, too. You see, after we bought the supplies and got the apartment keys from Brad's roommate, we went on our own fishing expedition.

We let ourselves in to Brad's place and I watched as Charley assembled the supplies — an eight-foot length of one-inch PVC pipe, some string and a magnet — into a kind of fishing pole. With this design, he figured he could "fish" for the keys, which were on the roof just above Brad's window. Charley removed the window screen and I went outside into the parking lot to direct him.

Charley would "cast" out the window, up over his head and backward, landing the magnet on the roof and I would tell him which way to drag the line, to "snag" the keys. "A little to your left...that's it now come straight down...nope. You missed 'em. Nope. Now you need to go a little to the right."

By the fourth cast Charley was ever so close to his prey. "Easy now, keep going, keep going, a little more...You're right on top of them! You've got 'em!"

Then, like a proud fisherman, Charley carefully "reeled in" his catch. He dragged the keys, "hooked" by the magnet, carefully down the roof, over the rain gutter and out over the parking lot, three stories up — proudly displaying his 2 ounce catch.

It was a great moment. And, although it was the smallest catch of the day, I think it was the best!

Chapter Four

Learning Lessons

*There's only a slight
difference between
keeping your chin up and
sticking your neck out—
but it's worth knowing.*

—Anonymous

Have we got a deal for you!

"It's old and not very pretty," we told the prospective buyer of our used, top-loading dishwasher. "But it still runs well. Besides where can you get a portable dishwasher these days for $25?"

Nowhere! We knew that because we'd been shopping for one for weeks. Like everything else, there are several different brands, styles, and prices from which to choose. Maybe, we thought, the best thing to do would be to get rid of our old dishwasher, first. Then we'd have room for a new one and a little extra cash to boot.

The appliance store would take our old one in trade. They'd give us a $30 credit toward a new one. "What will you do with our old one?" I asked. "It would go to the landfill. There's really no market for ones like that."

Why, that old dishwasher was practically part of the family! We couldn't just dump it in the landfill. We wanted it to go where it would be appreciated.

So, we decided to sell it for what we paid for it -- $25. We bought it used three years ago and used it until last year. It still works, although I did see a few drops of water on the floor after we performed a test run last week. Charley said the seal was probably a little dry from lack of use. It would more than likely take care of itself. But, we'd make sure we told her about it.

Her name was Judy. Judy had always wanted a dishwasher but could never afford one. When she learned about our $25 dishwasher she called us and made an appointment to come over and take a look.

Since she'd never owned a dishwasher before, we showed her how to attach it to the faucet, where to put the soap, and how to load the dishes. "It'll do the job," I assured her.

"It may have a small leak in the bottom," Charley said. "We suspect the seal around the motor, but that can easily be fixed."

"I can ask my brother to take a look at that," Judy said. "It looks good to me," she grinned from ear to ear. "I'll take it."

Not knowing who should get the money, Judy laid a $5 bill and a $20 bill on the table between us. Charley took the $5 bill off the table and returned it to Judy, saying, "Take this back just in case you need to have that seal fixed."

"Thank you," she said, touching the dishwasher gently, as if it were a precious family heirloom. I knew we had found the right home for it.

"I brought my son's car, it's got a hatch back," she said.

Charley said it would be best to load the dishwasher from the front porch. But the steps were snow covered. "I'll go shovel," Charley said. "You two wait inside where it's warm."

While we waited, I made the usual small talk. Had she lived here long?

She had lived in the area most of her life, at least since she was six years old. She moved back in with her parents when her son was born. And, now she was going back to school to get her high school diploma. If all goes as planned, she'll graduate next spring. Her son will graduate from high school the following year.

Did she work where Charley works? Is that how she found out about our dishwasher? No, she's not working right now. Her sister works there, saw the ad in the employee newsletter, and called her. Her sister couldn't understand why she wanted an old dishwasher.

As she talked about her life and how she was turning it around, a little voice inside me was saying, *Give her back the $20 and just let her take the dishwasher.*

So, I told Judy to wait just a minute and ran out to the porch. "Charley, I think we should just give her the dishwasher."

"What?" he said, looking up from his work. He hadn't had the benefit of hearing her life's story, as I had. "We gave her $5 back for the leak. That's fair."

Unsatisfied, I went back inside. Charley finished the steps and told Judy to bring the car around. As she did, the little voice inside my head persisted, *Give her the $20 back.*

About then Charley called for me to come and help them load the dishwasher. It was bulky but with the three of us maneuvering it, we managed to get most of it loaded. With three-quarters of it in, Judy needed to rest. She was in a car accident the week before, had hit her head on the windshield and hurt her arm.

Now the voice inside me was screaming, ***Give her the $20 back!*** I looked at Charley but he hadn't heard it.

We finished loading the dishwasher. She closed the hatch, turned, and thanked us for the wonderful buy. She was so pleased. I looked Charley's way for some kind of sign. He just smiled politely and said, "You're welcome. We hope you enjoy it."

Time was running out. Judy was moving toward the car door. I had to think of something. So, I asked Charley, "Did you know that Judy's gone back to school to get her diploma?" Judy took the cue. She told Charley about her impending graduation and that of her son's. "We expect to read about you in the paper," I told her.

Then I looked to Charley one more time, as Judy headed for the driver's seat. He looked at me and whispered, "Do you think we need to give Judy an early graduation present?"

That was all I needed. "Keep her here," I blurted out as I turned, bounded up the front steps, threw open the front door — letting in a cat — ran through the living room and dining room with my snow-covered boots, retrieved the $20 from the table and bounded back to Judy's son's car, which was now idling.

She rolled down the window and I placed the $20 bill in her hand. "Here," I said, "We want you to buy something special for yourself when you graduate."

Surprised, she protested momentarily then took the $20 and said, "Thank you!" with that big grin, "I will."

She waved, drove out of the yard and down the road. I turned to Charley with an even bigger grin. "Thank you!" I said.

"That's okay," he replied. "Judging by that sad look on your face, I didn't have much of a choice. Just do me a favor, the next time we want to **sell** something, let **me** handle it."

Things we learned on our summer vacation

Every year, when Charley has a week off from work because his office is closed down, I take the week off, too, and we pick one household project to complete. This year, it was improving our main (and only) bathroom.

In our century-plus farmhouse, the original "restroom" was an outside wooden structure featuring a door with a crescent moon. Indoor plumbing wasn't part of the floor plan when the house was originally built in 1887. So, we figure the 5 ½' x 7' room that houses our current indoor facilities was a converted pantry. It compactly accommodates one tub, one toilet, one sink, and has a little room left over for one occupant.

The ceramic tile on the walls is in good shape. But the floor is a combination of 50-year-old gray and white grouted tile, patches of cement that were applied to cover up old holes and an oblong piece of plywood that covers up the largest, most recent hole. The actual floor area covered by tile is only 3' x 7'. Judging by the square footage, re-tiling the converted pantry should have been a small part of the project.

There is no such thing as a small project. But, in order to re-tile the bathroom, we needed to remove the sink and toilet so we could replace the sub-floor before laying the tile. But, we couldn't remove the toilet until we had another one somewhere else on the premises. And, since we didn't want to resurrect the outdoor one with the crescent moon, Charley and I decided to install a temporary toilet in the basement — nothing fancy, just something that could be used until we got the bathroom floor tiled.

Sometimes you have to back up and take a run at it. Charley knew right where the temporary toilet would go. He'd been thinking about it for a while. The only problem was, we either needed to jackhammer out a section of the concrete basement floor to get the pipe low enough so it would drain properly or we needed to build the toilet up high enough to get good drainage. Not owning a jackhammer (although Charley would have bought one in a second, if I'd weakened) we opted for building the toilet up.

Charley figured out the design and said we needed some lumber. But before we could haul it, Charley needed to tune up the ol' truck, otherwise we might not make it to the store. So he bought new spark plugs, installed them and, finally, we were on our way to the local home-project warehouse store to get supplies for our temporary toilet project.

You can never have enough supplies. In fact, we went there on Saturday to get plumbing supplies, like elbows and connectors and pipe, on Sunday for a free lesson on how to install ceramic tile (remember the bathroom floor?), on Wednesday to return plumbing items that didn't fit and to buy lumber, on Friday to buy a toilet, and twice the next Saturday, once to get more lumber and a few small items and a second time to retrieve the bag of small items I'd forgotten at the cash register. (I may have forgotten them on purpose…early signs of home-project-store addiction.)

You need the right tools. We brought home the supplies and dove into our secondary project — the temporary toilet. Charley was the designer and builder and I was the gopher and quality-control inspector. He'd measure and cut and pound and I'd hold the light, check things with the level, and locate tools.

And, of course, in any home improvement project, you need the right tools for the job. You need tools to cut with, like hack saws, zip saws, jig saws, radial arm saws, circular saws, and hand saws. You need tools to make holes with, like hole saws and drills with multiple sizes of drill bits, including a brand new, super-duper 2 and 9/16" one, like real plumbers use. And, you need things that fasten things to other things, like screws, nails, glue, connectors, and lengths of pipe.

Not all plumbing pipe is created equal. Speaking of pipe, after several trips to the home-project store and one emergency trip to the handy hardware store around the corner, we discovered that not all plumbing pipe is the same. You've got your PVC and CPVC pipe, not to mention your Schedule 30 and Schedule 40 sizes. The long and short of it is, some are wider than others. Which is exactly what we discovered after we had shut off the water to the house and sawed the water line in half. Seems the pipe was one size and the connector was another. The good news was we made it to the hardware store just before they closed the doors for the night.

Just because it fit once doesn't mean it will fit again. Thank goodness they had the right size connector or we would've been without water for the evening. This experience has given us new appreciation for plumbers. Using the right size pipe, then getting pipes to fit together at the proper angle and in the proper way, is an art. And, then, after you have them together, you have to take them apart to glue them. And believe you me, when you put them together again for the final time, they don't always fit the same way...or so I've heard.

When glue says it sets in 30 seconds...believe it.

And, how about that plumber's cement? I've never seen such fast acting stuff. It says it sets in 30 seconds and I'm here to tell you it does. Oh, and by the way, it also bonds to other things just as quickly…like exposed skin.

Some vacations aren't necessarily restful. Well, after seven fun-filled days of learning, shopping, measuring, cutting, squatting, eyeballing, leveling, fitting, lifting, gluing, hammering, sawing, pounding, nailing, un-nailing, tightening, loosening, and re-tightening, we almost finished the temporary toilet. All it needs is a water supply, so we can flush. But that along with our real project, the bathroom, will have to wait a while longer because our week's vacation is at an end.

…Yup, it went right down the toilet…*almost*.

It's all in your head!

The home health care nurse told me that she'd have to poke my finger to get the five drops of blood they needed to run a test for the insurance application. I had put on a good face until now. I welcomed her to the farm; chatted with her about her kids, her work history, and her new career in home health care; discovered she likes dogs and that she had her last child at age 33.

I even learned she was going to Orlando for the weekend. I stalled as long as I could. But, the inevitable had come. She was about to poke me with a sharp instrument and draw blood.

"Which hand do you write with?" she asked. "I'm right-handed, why?" "This'll be sore for a few days and I don't want to slow you down." "Well, I use both hands to type. I guess that means I don't have to do this. Right?" She laughed. She thought I was kidding.

"This'll be over in a few minutes," she assured me. "Let's see your left hand." As I surrendered my left hand, I could feel myself beginning to get warm. *You'd better tell her,* I thought. *No, I can handle this,* I protested. Then, I heard myself say "Ouch!" She had gone and done it. She had poked me and was milking my finger as if it were a cow's udder.

My temperature began to rise. As I struggled with my right hand to remove my cardigan sweater, I began to feel light headed and clammy.

"I suppose I should tell you I don't do this sort of thing very well. It happens all the time. I feel so silly. I know it's all in my head," I said.

As she looked up from my finger to my face, she noticed I had turned a dull shade of gray. "I think you'd better lie down on the couch," she said.

"No, really I'm all right. We're almost through aren't we?" "No," came the answer. "I'm sorry to say but you're not bleeding." "What?" I moaned. "I can't get even one good drop of blood before it starts clotting. I'm going to have to poke you again."

My heart sank. "In that case, I think I'd like to lie down," I said with a forced smile.

By this time Charley had come in from walking the dogs and took over holding the cold wash cloth that was on my forehead. "She even does this when other people are giving blood. Like the time I was in the hospital a few years back, they were taking blood from me and **she** almost passed out."

"Thanks for sharing that, dear." I said. "Ouch!"

Then I asked the nurse who was now milking the second jab, "Where were you last week when I had that crack in my hand that wouldn't stop bleeding? How come I'm not gushing now?"

"You were relaxed then. Now your sympathetic nervous system has taken over. Your body is reacting to your mind and it's shutting off the blood flow," she explained. My mind was definitely in control of the situation because after half an hour and four finger pokes (including one on my right hand), she never did get the five little drops she needed.

"What now?" I inquired. "We'll send in what we've got and hope for the best," she said. "And, if that's not enough?" I probed. "I'll probably be back to find a vein," she said.

"No offense, but I hope I don't see you again," I responded, disappointed at my unintentional lack of blood flow. But, as I watched her drive away, I began to realize it wasn't unintentional.

I'd been preparing myself for this visit all week. I told myself how much I was dreading it. I reinforced that I didn't do the needle thing well, and, guess what? My mind programmed my body accordingly. Talk about power.

So, what if I put this awesome power to work in reverse? Instead of being apprehensive about that presentation I have to make to 9th and 10th graders, what if I tell myself how fun it will be, how much I'll learn, the great opportunity I'll have to impact even one young person, and the chance I'll get to meet new people. Will enthusiasm flow from me?

Instead of lamenting that the refrigerator has too much stuff in it and that I have to clean it out, what if I think how great it is that I have a house that has a refrigerator that has food in it. Will productivity flow from me?

Instead of wishing for thoughtful little things that my family could do for me, what if I think how thankful I am that I have a family and concentrate on the thoughtful little things I can do for them? Will harmony flow from me?

And, instead of thinking I don't do the needle thing well, what if I think to myself I love to watch the TV show *ER,* so I must be able to tolerate needles, doctors, and nurses. Will blood flow from me?

...O.K., so maybe this theory doesn't hold true for every case. But, my head says it's worth a try.

How about yours?

Getting a grip.

I've gotten into this habit of staying late at work on Friday nights. Charley's usually off at a ballgame somewhere so he's not waiting at home for me. And, it's quiet at the office. Mostly it's just the custodians and a few other stragglers who are trying to get "caught up." Which, of course, you never can do.

What with that stack of mail to sort through, routed newsletters and journals waiting to be read, voice mail to hear, e-mail to read, a "to-do" list that only seems to grow and urgencies that bubble up during the day, a person might never get caught up.

As usual, last Friday night I was in my office getting re-acquainted with my paper recycling bin when Tim, one of the night custodians, stuck his head in my door and said, "Hey busy lady, if you want to see something neat, stop across the street on your way home. One of our teachers and his wife are throwing a Halloween costume party for the kids."

The "building across the street" is the school that we run for special students – ones who have disabilities. And the "kids" are teenagers through young adults, who are in our classes, have completed the program or have turned 26. (Michigan law allows them to go to school through age 26.)

I smiled, said thanks for the tip and went back to my sorting. I was determined to get to the bottom of this pile and then I was going home. I was tired. It was after dark. And I was off duty. I finished sorting through the stack, packed up my stuff and got in my car. As I neared the building across the street, I saw cars in the lot and heard dance music. I had no intention of stopping. Then my car pulled over to the curb.

So, I got out, entered the building, found the darkened, music-filled cafeteria, and maneuvered past dancing goblins, witches, TV characters, and 19th century street urchins. I asked one urchin if she could help me find Mr. Douglas, the teacher. She said yes and led me to a tall, dark-haired monster dressed in surgical scrubs. He sported a squared-off head, platform shoes that made him a good six inches taller than usual, a stethoscope and a name badge that said Dr. Frank N. Stein. I would never have recognized him.

"Great costume!" I said above the din.

"Thanks," he said. "I enjoy getting dressed up as much as the kids do."

"Great party, too," I added.

"Yeah, my wife, Sandy and I get a kick out of seeing the kids have a good time," he said, smiling as he looked over the crowded dance floor. "There aren't many opportunities for them like this."

Just then, a young man approached me, shook my hand and said, "My name is Adam. Would you like to dance?" I noted that he had a strong handshake.

"I'd love to dance, Adam," I said.

He extended his hands and I put mine in his and noticed that same firm grip. We mostly swayed to the music about an arms-length away from each other. Every once in a while, Adam would decide it was time to twirl and we'd both go around. In between we made small talk. Adam wasn't shy.

"Do you know who I am?" Adam asked, referring proudly to his costume.

"No, who are you?" I asked, playing along.

"See, I'm wearing my Tae Kwon Do clothes. I'm a Tae Kwon Do master," he said.

"Oh, yes, of course you are," I said.

"I'm 24 years old. Are you 24, too?" Adam asked.

"No, I'm a few years older than that," I smiled, flattered — until I considered the innocent source and darkened room.

"I have two more years of school, unless they change the law. My teacher is Jack Strong. Do you know Jack Strong? I like him. Do you know my teacher assistants Val, Barb and Lenny? Lenny – he's new. I take adult ed classes on Tuesday. My favorite movie star is Jim Carrey. I like Jim Carey."

"You look a lot like Jim Carrey. Did anyone ever tell you that, Adam?"

"Lots of people. I have a job. I wash dishes at The Pasta Place. I love my job."

All the while Adam was talking his hands were closed tightly around mine. And when we twirled he didn't loosen them to allow for movement. I was afraid something was going to snap.

"Can we dance without holding hands for a minute?" I asked, hoping for some relief.

"I need to hold on, so I don't lose you," Adam said maintaining his grip and continuing to sway with the music.

Deciding not to focus on my squashed knuckles, I asked, "Where do you live, Adam?"

"I live in Ann Arbor. Do you know where Ann Arbor is?"

"Yes," I said.

"Where do you live?" Adam asked.

"I live about half an hour north of here."

"Do you live near Flint? My aunt lives in Flint. My mom and I go visit my aunt. I stay with her sometimes in the summer. Do you have kids?"

"Yes, we have two," I said.

"It's just my mom and me now. I don't have any brothers and sisters. I might take driver's ed someday. Yeah. Someday maybe. Is this Aerosmith? It sounds like them. Hey, who are you?" Adam had spotted Mr. Douglas.

"Dr. Frank N. Stein. You know, Frankenstein the monster. Arrrggghhh!" Mr. Douglas said.

"Oh yeah. You're funny," Adam laughed.

The song was over and suddenly I remembered I was tired.

"Thanks for the dance, Adam. I have to go now," I said.

"OK," he said, abruptly releasing my hands, turning away and asking the next young lady who passed by to dance.

I watched Adam for a minute swaying on the dance floor. Then I turned back to Dr. Frank N. Stein, said goodnight and headed for my car. As I drove north, I worried about all the things I didn't get done at work and all the things that were waiting for me at home. I could feel my hands grip the steering wheel with increasing intensity.

Then I thought about Adam. My grip relaxed and a smile spread across my face. He's a special young man all right. He may have some disabilities but he also has some gifts. He knows when it's time to hang on tight…and when it's time to let go.

Be careful what you wish for...

It's part of Charley's job to evaluate new cars. So, he gets different vehicles assigned to him throughout the year. Usually it's fun to travel in them but the current one is a compact, stripped down, economy model with a truck-like ride. It's reliable enough, but to be truthful, I was dreading our 800-mile trip to Missouri over Memorial weekend in the vehicle I had nick-named the "tin can." I was really wishing we had a nicer car to drive.

Just as I was packing my kidney belt for the long ride, Charley pulled into the driveway with a luxury car that had 85 miles on it. It had a soft suspension, plush interior, daytime running lights, on-board satellite location system, digital radio, 10 CD changer, air bags, reclining leather bucket seats, compass, cup holders – the works. It was his newly assigned vehicle and was everything I had wished for.

With new enthusiasm for the road trip, I finished packing and we shoved off. We had a pleasant ride south (once we figured out how to work the radio!). But after 12 hours and 800 miles, even the plushest car can feel cramped. We were glad to turn off the highway onto the dirt road that led to Charley's boyhood home in Selmore. We were excited to see his dad, Marvin, Marvin's sister, Aunt Margie (who now lives at the farm since Uncle Sherman passed), Miss Kitty (the feline in charge) and to stretch our legs.

Thankfully, over the next few days our car travel was limited to short trips: to the church cemetery to visit Charley's family, to the next town to see 96-year-old Grandma, and to a town "down the road" to visit Grandma's cousin and to decorate graves there. We were saving up for the big trip on Sunday to Lynchburg where Marvin, Margie and their five siblings grew up – about 1½ hours away.

Every Memorial Day (or Decoration Day as they call it), all the aunts and uncles and cousins gather for a potluck lunch and then go to the cemetery to decorate grandma and grandpa's grave. It's a special time to remember those who have gone before, to bond with those who are there, and to pass along family history to the younger generation.

Marvin offered his 1988 Cadillac for the Lynchburg trip, but Charley said we'd take the new car. "It'll save wear and tear on the Caddy." So we loaded the food and silk flowers into the trunk, settled into the leather seats, and set off on our journey. We stopped twice on the way, once for free coffee at the rest area and once to visit Uncle Sherman at the New Hope cemetery.

We left New Hope and arrived in Lynchburg in time for lunch. We ate, hugged, visited, decorated the graves, shared childhood stories, said our good-byes, and roared down the road with our 32-valve engine. We had one more stop to make in very rural country before we headed the 20 miles back to the main highway and the 70 miles back home.

Aunt Margie needed a sewing machine from the farm where she and Uncle Sherman had lived. So, we wound our way through the back roads and woods and across Dunnigan's bridge (the one that crosses the creek by old man Dunnigan's place) to the 380-acre farm, loaded the sewing machine in the trunk and drove toward downtown Falcon. We had just passed the post office, **the one and only building** in downtown Falcon, when it happened.

I heard a gurgling noise and Charley began wrestling with the steering wheel. "What's wrong?" Marvin asked from the back seat. "I think we threw a belt," Charley said. "The power steering's gone." Within seconds, the on-board LCD display scrolled across the dashboard flashing "Battery not charging...battery not charging..." and the air conditioning quit.

Decision time. Do we stop here in "downtown" Falcon on the Sunday of Memorial weekend, where there is no sign of life? Or, do we try to make it home? Hmmm. The temperature gauge was normal. The engine wasn't overheating. And, we were still moving. If we stopped, we might not get started again.

We decided to risk it. We turned off the radio and anything else electrical that we could, rolled down the windows, put the pedal to the metal and hoped for the best. The goal was to get as close to Selmore as possible. Then we'd use the car phone to call for help.

As we watched the odometer log mile after mile, each one bringing us closer to Selmore, we grew more confident. Like Marvin said, "It doesn't take much juice to keep a car running." But, just when we thought we'd make it, the high-tech features on the car began to conspire against us. The on-board computer decided it was time to give us more warnings about our loss of power. First, there were more messages flashing across the dash. Then, there were messages **plus** warning bells that began to sound. And, of course, we couldn't find a button or knob to turn off those *%!# automatic daytime running lights. They were all sucking up our limited electrical reserve.

35. 40. 45. 50. The odometer ticked away the miles, as we wondered where we'd be forced to stop. We made the turn toward Springfield, about 20 miles from Selmore. "Anything after this is gravy," Charley announced, above the now constantly ringing warning bells. As the final warning

message, "Battery has no reserve…" flashed across the dash, we answered back in frustration, "WE KNOW! Just hang on a little longer!"

We headed up one hill and down the other side, gaining a little speed. Unfortunately the next hill was even bigger. As we crested the hill, all systems went dark. Not one LCD display was lit and (thankfully) the warning bells stopped. As the dashboard went blank, the car began to miss and jerked down the last hill as we headed toward Selmore. Then everything stopped and we began to coast. Charley gripped the steering wheel and guided us slowly, silently off the highway onto the Selmore turn-off and we rolled to a stop – ¾ of a mile from the farm!

We whooped and cheered and congratulated ourselves at nearly making it home. Marvin jumped out of the luxury car, walked to the farm, got the 1981 pick-up, drove back and jumped the silent 1998 vehicle so Charley could drive it back to the farm. Aunt Margie and I chose to ride back to the farm in the **more reliable transportation** – the pick-up.

The car was repairable but we had to extend our stay in Missouri a few extra days. Seems the model was too new for the dealership to have the part. They had to send away for it. By Wednesday, it was ready.

We picked up the car at the dealership in Springfield about 2 p.m. As we were leaving the parking lot, we came upon a guy struggling to maneuver his mint-condition, 1960 pick-up out of a parking spot.

Charley motioned for him to go ahead. As he passed, Charley said, "Nice truck!" The driver grinned back and said through his open window, "Thanks, but at times like this, I wish it had power steering!"

As we left the parking lot headed for Michigan, I turned to Charley and said, "If I were him, I'd be careful what I wished for…"

Have you got change?

Change: The only person who enjoys it is a wet baby.

I'm living proof. It takes a lot for me to change and it's even worse when it's forced on me. Take my grocery store, for instance. I've shopped there since moving to the farm eight years ago. It's not the most glamorous of stores, but it's on the way home and it's comfortable. And, for eight years I've known where all of my favorite products are on every shelf.

But, last week when I walked in, everything was changed! The produce was rearranged. The canned goods were shuffled from aisles on the west side of the store to aisles on the east side. And some of the aisles were missing, replaced by tables arranged in an open-air display. I had dashed in for a few items and was lost in what used to be a familiar place.

Change comes hard.

What should have taken me 10 minutes took half an hour because I had to really look at what was on each shelf. I muttered, "I hate this," as I pushed my cart through the unfamiliar displays. Why the change? "Competition," the cashier said. "A new, super grocery store is moving in up the street. So, we're remodeling."

No one consulted me about the change. If they had, I would have said, "Don't do it!" I don't care about the superstore soon to be moving in up the street. Today I just care about finding some produce, a can of soup and a loaf of bread. Spending quality time in the grocery store is not high on my list of leisure-time priorities.

Change makes you work.

When my boss was 14 years old, he and a few other boys were chosen to do summer custodial work at his school. Mrs. Clark, the custodial matron, had them cleaning floors, windows and toilets. She kept her young charges busy every minute they were on the clock. It was hard work, but my boss was thankful to have a paying job.

One day, after the boys had been cleaning the bathrooms for awhile, they felt they needed a break. So, it was decided that my boss would be the spokesperson and, at the right moment, he would make that request of Mrs. Clark. When Mrs. Clark came to check on their progress, my boss saw his opportunity and said, "Mrs. Clark, we're tired. We sure could use a rest." To that Mrs. Clark responded, "I'll tell you what boys, let's go clean some windows instead. A change is as good as a rest." And, off they went.

Change surprises you.

My boss internalized Mrs. Clark's philosophy of change as rejuvenating and practiced it throughout his work life. So, when he was reminiscing about his 37-year career in our industry at a recent staff meeting and then announced that he would be "retiring" from his job and changing to another, it made perfect sense but caught everyone off guard. Our staff sat in stunned silence as he broke the news. And, many are still wrestling with the realization that he'll be leaving soon.

At first, I hated the idea. (He obviously didn't consult me before making his decision to leave.) From my perspective, he's been a good boss (he's my immediate supervisor) and a good leader for our agency these last 13 years. So why mess with a good thing? I guess he figures it's better to go out when you're at the top of your game.

Change is inevitable.

Last week our Board of Directors regretfully accepted my boss's request to retire. (Once again, no one consulted me.) Then, they interviewed and selected his successor…the number 2 man who's been a part of the management team for 11 years. (And, of course, no one consulted me. There's a pattern here…) The number 2 (soon to be number 1) man has definite ideas of his own. He'll be carrying out the Board's goals but will be doing it in his own style. And, that will result in changes for a lot of us. He'll be evaluating his staff needs, making adjustments, and asking us to do things differently. It can be scary, if you choose to see it that way.

Change is as good as a rest.

But, as I reflect on the opportunity of doing new things, I'm intrigued. The thought of learning new skills or using existing skills in new ways could be exciting, yes, even rejuvenating. I've been at my job for nearly 12 years and everything once familiar could be rearranged much like my grocery store. It could be like working in a new place.

Change adds spice to life.

I visited my grocery store again last week with a different mind set. I allowed some extra time to stroll through the aisles. And while I was looking for the old familiar stand-by products, I also found a few new ones to try. They'll add a little zip to our diet.

Change helps you grow.

Maybe that's another reason babies like it.

Change: Bring it on.

Having a ball?

I'm athletically challenged. I've known it since I was young. Over the years, I've learned to accept it. But, as part of being a kid, you have to participate in games. So, I put in just enough effort with tag, Red Rover, softball, basketball and miniature golf to be part of the group. I breathed a sigh of relief when I was older and could do other things in my free time that I really enjoy — like writing or spending time with people I like.

Then about 10 years ago, I found myself entered in a golf scramble. Charley, my sports-loving friend, had signed us up for the church's first annual golf event. I was petrified. I had successfully avoided sports-like activities for nearly 20 years. And now I was going to play golf? I had never been on a real golf course. I had only played miniature golf — badly. I had every right to be nervous.

To my relief, when the day of the scramble came, we played "best ball." In best ball, all four of the players on your team (called a foursome) take their best shot and you get to choose from which of the four spots to hit your next ball. With this kind of arrangement you don't have to be good, you just have to show up. The scramble rules said you had to use a few of everyone's shots and we did use a of few of mine. But mostly I would hit my ball, pick it up and go to the spot where someone else on my team had made an awesome shot and hit my next ball from there.

I can do this, I thought. So, I bought a set of used golf clubs and became a regular at the annual church scramble.

Then, a few years ago, Pat, a friend from the American Business Women's Association, organized a women's golf league. *Heck*, I thought, *if I can do the church outing once a year, this once-a-week stuff should be even more fun.* So, I signed on.

The big day came. I arrived for my first league play and guess what? Scramble rules don't apply! When you play on a league, there is no best ball play. You have to hit your own ball, wherever it lies. *What? No more team play? Well, this could slow down my game considerably.*

And, it has. On some holes for every stroke that others on my foursome take, I take two. Fortunately, my teammates are patient with my duffs, whiffs, dribbles, slices, hooks, mulligans, and lost balls. They're humble, consistent, and kind competitors. They have fun, play their own game, and still encourage me. "Oh, don't worry, your next shot will be the one."

This year — even with all their support — I fell into a slump. I couldn't do anything right. "That's it," I told Charley. "At the end of the season, I'm hanging up my clubs. I'd do it now but I've already paid for the entire 14 weeks." (That was smart planning on the part of our league organizer.)

I might as well face it. After several years of non-improvement (not to mention the years of back-sliding) and lots of muttering and mumbling to myself, I've concluded that unlike my teammates, I will probably never be consistent, which means I will never be competitive. So why play golf?

Then, I remembered the other quality that my teammates share. They have fun. Why only last week after a terrible shot, a member of my foursome asked, "Are we having fun yet?"

Yeah, that's it. Maybe if I work at it, I can at least have fun.

Since then, things have been better. For the second week in a row, I've been relaxed, made good drives, good fairway shots, and done some pretty good pitching onto the green. I've even had a few good putts. Everyone on my team is amazed at the improvement (yours truly included). One of my teammates even suggested I should receive the most improved player award.

I don't know how long this streak will last. But, I'm enjoying it. I've been able to hit shots about as far and as straight as everyone else. Why, sometimes our shots have been clustered so closely together, it's as if we were playing best ball.

After this week's round, I felt good enough to go back to the clubhouse for dinner, a beverage, and to talk about my game with the others. The great shots, the whiffs, and the near misses all got analyzed.

Then we drifted to more personal topics. One member has felt the squeeze of corporate downsizing and is looking for a job. If she can't find a position in Michigan, she'll have to look out of state. I suppose coming back on Wednesdays for golf would be out of the question.

Another is considering taking her 11-year-old nephew to raise until he's 18. She hasn't had young children at home for nearly 20 years. Can she adjust her lifestyle to do it? Will she have to quit the league? Maybe we can help her find a baby-sitter for Wednesday nights.

One of our newest members is recently divorced and is now a single mom. While married, she and her husband played on a mixed golf league. When they divorced, he got custody of the mixed league, and she volunteered to join another. We're glad she found us.

As we talked and laughed about the game and the issues in our lives, I realized why I'll come back next year. It's not the game, although I hope some day to be a better golfer (maybe take a few lessons?). It's the people. Some of the nicest ones I know just happen to play golf.

Please be car-ful!

Monday, 8 a.m. "Wintry conditions continue in southeastern Michigan today but roads are clear and dry," the radio reports. Pat's driving. I'm riding shotgun. We're headed to work. She says she's been thinking about getting a new car. Hers is only two years old but the odometer reads 63,000 miles and there's no sense asking for trouble. Maybe she'll buy her mom's '97 with 19,000 miles on it.

8:50 a.m. We arrive at work pretty much on schedule. We agree to work through lunch (we usually do) and leave the office before 5 (we usually don't). The weatherman predicts snow. Last Friday it took us two hours to get home in that bumper-to-bumper mess.

3 p.m. I glance out my office window. It's snowing.

4:15 p.m. My daughter-in-law calls. "You need to leave work, soon. It's really snowing hard and I'm nervous about my drive home and I only have a few miles to go. Be careful."

4:30 p.m. Pat sticks her head in my office. She's just come from a meeting outside the building. "Roads are getting bad. Let's leave in 15 minutes and get out of the city before rush hour."

4:55 p.m. We brush half an inch of snow off Pat's car that's only been parked for 25 minutes. It's really coming down.

4:58 p.m. We pick up today's newspaper from the box in front of work. I'll read it to Pat during the long ride home.

5 p.m. We drive through residential streets, making our way to the expressway. It's snowing so hard, we have to open windows to watch for traffic at busy cross streets.

5:15 p.m. We're on the expressway entrance ramp.

5:16 p.m. We merge onto the expressway and reach a maximum cruising speed of 30 mph. Decent for road conditions.

5:17 p.m. I skim through the paper and begin to read a story aloud.

5:18 p.m. Pat interrupts …"I can't stop…I can't stop!" I look up from my reading and blurt out…"Pump your brakes…Pump your brakes!"

5:18 p.m. and 10 seconds. Pat's clutching the steering wheel and pumping the brakes as we approach the bridge – going downhill. It's a sheet of ice. There's a car stopped sideways on the expressway in front of us, blocking the right lane and part of the left. Pat's steering us into the left lane and pumping for all she's worth but we're accelerating and there's nowhere to go. The left shoulder on the bridge is usually wide enough to accommodate a car but right now it's occupied by a three-foot snow bank and backed by a cement barrier that separates the eastbound traffic from those like us going west.

5:18 p.m. and 30 seconds. No change in speed, Pat tries to graze the snow bank to slow us down. But the left front tire catches in the drift and we come to an abrupt halt – a safe distance away from the sideways car but not completely off the roadway.

5:18 p.m. and 40 seconds. We look at each other, exhale, and…

5:18 p.m. and 50 seconds. *Bang!* Someone hits us from behind. Our car spins around to face oncoming traffic.

5:19 p.m. As cars crawl by, we take stock. We're both shaken but whole thanks to our seatbelts. Pat bumped her head and I bumped my hip. We look out and see the van that hit us come to rest in the snow bank. Snow continues to fall.

5:19 p.m. and 30 seconds. The driver of the van appears at Pat's window. "I'm so sorry. I'm so sorry. Is everyone okay?" "Yes. Are you okay?" "Yes." "Let's see if you can move your car to the side of the road." He blocks traffic as Pat maneuvers us as close as she can to the shoulder. It gives us hope that the car is driveable. Still facing the wrong way, we're now nose to nose with his van.

5:21 p.m. While he and Pat lament that the car that caused the accident is long gone, I call 911 on the cell phone. "We're on the bridge headed westbound, where Burton Drive merges. No injuries. Two vehicles."

5:22 p.m. We decide to get out and survey the damage. Pat's door is jammed. He helps her get out. My door is fine. The back tire on the driver's side is pushed in at the top and sticks out at an angle on the bottom. The neck of the gas tank is protruding from the car's body. Traffic streams by, unaffected.

5:23p.m. We call a tow truck. "Call back when the police arrive."

5:24p.m. We wait for the police. A steady flow of cars, vans, SUVs, trucks and 18-wheelers *w-h-o-o-s-h* by within feet of each other and us.

5:30 p.m. We call our husbands. "Uhhh…We're going to be a little late getting home." It's dark and snowing harder. Two 18-wheelers zoom buy in tandem, their side mirrors nearly touching. There's a passenger car just ahead of them slowly merging onto to expressway. Air horns blare. We tense. The only thing that's protecting us from oncoming traffic is the van that hit us.

5:45 p.m. We call the nearest car dealership. "How late are you open?" "8 p.m." "Do you have any rental cars?" "No."

6 p.m. We wait...try to figure out how we're going to get home…

6:22 p.m. ...and wonder what's keeping the police. I did say westbound, didn't I?

6:44 p.m. When the van driver calls police to inquire about our promised assistance, he's told they've been re-routed to an injury accident. "It's a very busy night," the dispatcher explains.

6:53 p.m. A fire rescue truck *finally* arrives with lights flashing, followed by a police car. "Anyone want to go to the hospital?" "No, we just want to go home."

6:54 p.m. A firefighter calls the station and requests a load of sand for the bridge. "It's glare ice out here."

6:55 p.m. The officer asks us what happened and begins his report.

7:05 p.m. Pat and I are instructed to wait in the police car because "this one is going to be towed soon."

7:10 p.m. We gather our belongings and make our way against traffic in blowing snow to the police cruiser and plop ourselves down in the back seat. *Ouch!* There's no padding on the seat. It's just hard molded plastic. "That's so no one can stash anything back there," the officer informs us as he completes his report.

7:15 p.m. Never been in the back of a patrol car before. We check it out. Cold, hard, molded seats; a cage separating us from an officer with four years of experience resigned to traffic duty tonight; a shot gun in the front seat; a two-way radio broadcasting lots of chatter.

7:22 p.m. Tow truck arrives. Tow truck driver bends the front fender away from the van's front tire. The van drives away. Tow truck driver hooks up Pat's car and tows it.

7:30 p.m. "Where can I take you?" the officer asks. "Home? It's about 30 miles from here." "Pick some place closer," he says. Pat suggests her daughter Lara's apartment – about seven miles away. He agrees. It's still snowing. Pat calls her husband tells him where we're headed, asks him to call my husband and Lara.

7:45 p.m. Lara greets us, feeds us and encourages us to stay the night. "Otherwise, you'll just have to drive back down in this mess tomorrow morning. Besides, I can drive you to work." That's all the convincing we need. We call our husbands and tell them we'll see them tomorrow. Then we have a pajama party.

10:45 p.m. Fall into bed, exhausted.

Tuesday, 7:50 a.m. Lara drops us off at work.

10:30 a.m. Pat finds a rental car, after calling eight places.

11:30 a.m. She gets a ride to the rental car office and picks up the car. It's snowing again.

4:15 p.m. We're leaving work *early* today. It's still snowing and more is predicted. We brush snow from the rental car's windows.

4:17 p.m. We get in the nearly-new rental car and buckle up. We recall how just yesterday we were talking about Pat getting a new car. We laugh nervously and vow **never again** to talk about getting a new car during our commute!

Technical note: Pat didn't have anti-lock brakes and was correct to pump them. It's different for anti-lock brakes. What does your owner's manual say?

There's fire in the furnace!

Thursday evening after Election Day, we gathered on the west side of town at Diane's house for a potluck dinner to celebrate. The cause for which we had worked so tirelessly over the last five months was successful. The proposal was defeated. It was a victory for grass roots politics and an example of what a small group of determined people can do.

Diane led us in a toast to "Success!" We raised our glasses, "Here, here!" Then we filled our plates to overflowing. Balancing them ever so carefully on our laps, we sat in a circle in her living room rehashing the events leading up to election day and speculating about this most peculiar of General Elections, particularly the race for president.

That's when Sam reminded us that if the Electoral College process didn't result in the election of a president, Congress would have to step in and help choose the next leader of the free world. Bob wondered if it would be the lame duck Congress or the Congress that takes over in January?

Joe had stayed up late last night searching through the U.S. Constitution to discover that very answer. In fact, he could show us the exact passage because he happened to have a copy of the Constitution in his car right outside. Mid-mouthful, he ducked out to get it.

Now, I try to stay up on politics. I listen to talk radio, watch television news, read newspapers and news magazines. But, I'm an amateur compared to these hard-core politicos. Heck, I couldn't put my hands on a copy of the U.S. Constitution if my life depended on it, let alone know what a particular section says.

In an instant, Joe returned waving his copy of the document. "Here it is…right here in this section…" The party guests eagerly passed around the booklet, one by one, reading the passage, some interpreting it one way and others another. "But either way, we probably don't have to worry," Nick said. "The presidential race will be decided well before then."

Others agreed, it couldn't possibly come down to an act of Congress and the conversation shifted from the presidential race to the race for U. S. Senate—also a close one. As the speculation continued, I watched with wonder as their eyes brightened and their body language reflected their passion for politics.

This was exhilarating. Oh, I've been active in local school tax issues. And, I've attended public hearings of the local planning and zoning board and the township board. I've even written a few letters to the editor. But, this was the first time I'd worked on a campaign at the grass roots level, coming together with others I hadn't known to impact the political process.

I worked with Democrats, Republicans, Independents and the Greens. We might not have agreed on party politics, but, we agreed on the process: one person—one vote.

I was proud to be associated with such an energetic group of political activists. They worked tirelessly for five months, telling citizens about an issue they believed in. They
· submitted letters to the editor
· had a booth at every farmer's market

· held neighborhood coffees
· sent out informational mailings
· flew a banner over the football stadium
· ran ads in the newspaper
· handed out leaflets door-to-door
· made presentations to large and small groups
· wrote letters to friends
· put out yard signs
· encouraged people to register to vote

We all kept in touch through an e-mail list serve. June, our countywide chairperson, set it up. Not much gets by this seventy-something retired school teacher. When an issue needed clarification or a question needed an answer, I could count on a lively e-mail dialogue. Much of the traffic occurred after 10 p.m. when others with less fervor were off-line.

It would be common to come home from work and find 10 or 15 messages from members of the group on my home e-mail. It was a great way to stay in touch.

It's time now for dessert. June brings out a cake to help celebrate Scott's birthday. Scott served as one of the co-leaders on the east side of town. He and his wife, Mickey, dedicated much time and energy to the campaign. Scott sits swapping jokes with Virginia who is no slouch when it comes to knowing her mind and her politics. When he makes a remark she doesn't like, Virginia reminds Scott that she's his elder and should be respected. Virginia is 85. Scott is a mere 84.

As we sing happy birthday to Scott, I look around the room at the beaming faces of people who were strangers to me just five months ago. I see the faces of this group called the **Gray Panthers**. Faces encircled with gray hair. Faces adorned with laugh lines. Faces with bodies that don't move as quickly or as easily as they used to but can still get the job done. Faces that belong to individuals who have forgotten more than I'll ever know. Wise faces that tell me anything is possible, if I just put my mind to it.

Oh, there are a few younger faces in the room, ones that aren't eligible for membership in AARP. But for the most part, this core group of activists sports an average age of 75. Sharp, alert, and well versed in American government, they've proven

...that growing older means growing wiser.

...that "active senior" is more than a marketing term.

...that a small group of dedicated people, regardless
    of age, can make a big difference.

After dessert, the conversation moves easily from the current election to discussions about what's next on the political horizon. We can't let this momentum fade, we need to get busy on a new cause.

I feel my energy wane and my eye lids growing heavy. It's been a long day and it's getting late. I have to go to work tomorrow. I say my farewells and promise to keep in touch.

As I walk out the door, these tireless seniors are buzzing about the next hot topic. And I hear one of them say, "That's why they call us the Gray Panthers, because we're ready to pounce on issues like this."

And, I have no doubt they will. I close the door, head out into the darkness and say to the stars, "When I grow up, I want to be just like them!"

There may be snow on the roof but there's fire in the furnace. And, they're about to turn up the heat.

CHAPTER FIVE

LEAVING HOPE

*Nothing helps a man more
than knowing someone has
faith in him.*

—Anonymous

Everyday heroes

I've only seen Mrs. Dennison a couple of times. Besides being the mother of my friend, Jan, and knowing that we both enjoy writing, I don't really know much about her. And, I hardly recognized her when she stepped out of the van.

She had come to pick up the flowers she'd ordered from our annual business women's flower sale. "Jan's in class today," Mrs. Dennison announced as she gave me a hug. "She's determined to get that degree."

"Good for her," I said. "But, we're still glad to see you. We've got your order right over here." As we loaded her flats of annuals and hanging baskets, Mrs. Dennison inquired about my writing, "Jan told me you had one of your articles published recently." "Yes," I smiled proudly, "in Metro Woman Magazine."

"That's great," she said. "Do you belong to a writer's group? There's one in Lansing that has wonderful workshops. I go whenever I can," she offered.

"Sounds interesting. I'd love to learn more about it. Does this mean you're getting serious about your writing?" I asked.

"Well, no — not really. I always intended to do more writing after I retired. But, I need a computer that's not from the Stone Age. The one I have is from Jan's old office and it can't run the programs I'm used to using.

"I guess that's a poor excuse," she continued. "I can order a new computer. It's the other stuff going on at home..." her eyes began to well with tears. "The kids don't want to hear it, but I think something's wrong with their dad. It's his memory—he's showing signs of dementia. Our doctor suspects mini strokes..."

Just then, one of the other sale workers hollered, "Hey Gerri...Your dad's here to pick up his flowers." I signaled that I'd be right there. I couldn't leave Mrs. Dennison in mid-sentence.

"...and then I have my handicapped brother to look after..." her voice trailed off. She wasn't looking for sympathy. She just wanted to tell someone she was feeling overwhelmed and perhaps even a little scared.

Lamely, I offered, "Maybe if you write about your experiences, it might help others."

"I don't think I can...it's too close," she said, the tears returning.

Any other bright ideas? I asked myself.

"Geraldine Luella!" This time it was my dad motioning me over. I **had** to go. As a final clumsy thought I offered, "Maybe you can write it down for yourself...you know...just to get the feelings out."

Her eyes still moist, she now realized I had to get back to the sale. I gave her a hug and told her I'd be looking forward to getting the writer's group information. She got in her van and pulled away but her story stayed behind. It lingered through the rest of the morning and followed me home, competing for my attention as other examples of everyday heroes bombarded my thoughts.

There's Brett, the father of two young girls, whose marriage is ending. His wife has moved out and now he's Mr. Mom. He's learned what throwing a birthday party for a four-year-old involves. He's preparing their new house to be sold, taking care of his two pre-school-age girls, cleaning the house, mowing the yard, and trying to keep up at work. He admits some days are better than others.

And, what about Margaret? A single woman, she's dividing her time between her mother's house and her elderly aunt's home, trying to keep both places running. She didn't buy any flowers this year — even though she loves them. "There's just no time to plant them," she said, offering a forced smile, then fixing her gaze on something over my shoulder rather than look me in the eye.

We hardly saw Kate this year. Her pre-teen nephew lived with her for a few months. Her mother and father spent five months at her house. Her mother-in -law and father-in-law were both ill and she took care of them until they passed away. And, now she spends her Saturdays trying to sell her in-laws mobile home. She's weary. She threatened once to pack the van and leave. But she didn't.

Pam and Dan are caring for Dan's 93-year-old mother. They moved her to their house when they discovered she wasn't eating properly because she "fired" all the Meals on Wheels volunteers. They both work, and it's getting harder to leave mom home alone because she's disoriented. They found an opening at an aided-care facility close-by and took mom to lunch there. She said it was a nice place to visit but it could never be home. They're not sure what to do.

Bonnie is a married, 17-year-old with an 18-month-old son. Bonnie, her son and husband live with Bonnie's mother and younger brother. Her father died about two years ago. Each weekday morning, Bonnie drops her son off at day care before she heads to high school. In the afternoon, she works a part-time job where she's learning to be a secretary. In the evening, she helps her mother with the house. She rarely misses work. Last week I asked her how old she was and she said, "Seventeen … going on 30."

Mrs. Dennison, Brett, Margaret, Kate, Pam, Dan and Bonnie are everyday people. They're not perfect. They wonder aloud about the choices they have to make or feel cheated by the lack of choices they have. But they keep on keepin' on. They hang in there. They keep the faith. They don't give up. That's what makes them heroes.

Perhaps *you're* an everyday hero – quietly, consistently doing the best *you* can in a difficult situation. On behalf of those you help, **thank you**.

And when you're feeling used up, give yourself credit for the good you're doing. Cherish small victories. Know that you're making a difference. Treat yourself kindly. Pray. Share your burden. Be brave. Laugh.

Take care of yourself. The world has need of you!

One day at a time

What'll it be today?...Do I feel like a tuna on whole wheat or a corned beef on rye? Or maybe just a plain ol' grilled cheese on white!

So this is what it feels like to be a member of the sandwich generation. I had no idea until about two months ago.

That's when Dad began to have his problems. They're not life threatening and for that we're thankful. But they are taking their toll.

My Dad has been fortunate. Except for back surgery at age 84, he's never had anything more serious than a cold. But since he's celebrated [in his words] the 50th anniversary of his 39th birthday, things aren't as easy as they used to be. And, he's still not feeling right even after two trips to the emergency room and several follow-up visits with his doctor. And, when he's feeling his worst, he calls us for help.

So, for the past two months, my younger brother, Bill, and I have been conditioned—like Pavlov's dogs—to switch into emergency response mode whenever a telephone rings.

After a few weeks of being "on call," we decided it would be best for everyone if we spent more time with Dad. At first, we took turns spending entire days with him.

Rise at 6 a.m. Bring in the newspaper. Drink orange juice. Eat corn flakes. Take pills. Take a shower. Call Julie (Dad's girlfriend). Take the newspaper over to Julie. Go to the bank. Go to the drug store. Get the car washed. Come home. Have a snack. Turn on the computer. Check for e-mail. Listen to a taped church service. Call Julie. Have lunch. Answer the phone—it's the downstairs neighbor. Listen to Rush on the radio. Send an e-mail message to a granddaughter. Answer the phone—it's the upstairs neighbor. Watch a M*A*S*H rerun. Talk with the downstairs neighbor who has come upstairs to visit. Answer the phone—it's a friend from the senior center. Fix dinner. Eat dinner while watching the evening news. Watch *The Wheel of Fortune*— get puzzles right 50% of the time. Watch *Jeopardy!*—get questions right 10% of the time. Take pills. Answer the phone—it's one of my siblings. Watch cable "news/talk" show. Call Julie to say goodnight. Take one last pill. Turn in at 10:05 p.m. Get up several times during the night.

While these days go quickly, spending all day with Dad means I'm not at work. And, although family comes first, work needs attention, too. So, now we have a schedule. Bill has the day shift, and I have dinner and over-night duty. And, our three out-of-town siblings have phone duty, calling Dad daily or whenever they can.

During the week, I stay overnight at Dad's and go to work in the morning. So, Dad and I get up early, read the paper, eat cornflakes, bananas and milk or instant oatmeal with peaches. Then, while I shower Dad packs my lunch— usually some variation of a cheese sandwich, baby carrots, some potato chips, a cereal bar and an orange. [We've been calling it the 'boomerang orange' because I keep bringing it back every night and every morning it's back in my lunch.] I leave for work about 7:30 a.m. and call Dad around noon to see how things are going and to thank him for my delicious lunch. Then I head back there about 6 p.m.

After five weeks of living out of my car and making only brief stops at the farm to see my husband, stockpile his lunches and dinners, check the mail, do laundry, grocery shop, walk the dogs, and pay a few bills, I have a heightened appreciation for veteran caregivers. And, while being a sandwich-generation member is a few sandwiches short of a picnic, I'm beginning to see the positives in my altered, nomadic lifestyle.

- I have a wonderful husband, Charley, who supports me in doing what needs to be done!
- I talk with Charley more (but see him less....this may be a positive for him!!)
- I have an understanding boss who I really appreciate!
- I have supportive siblings who call Dad often.
- I'm glad I'm not an only child.
- I can floss at a moment's notice because my toiletries are always with me.
- The extra set of work clothes in my car comes in handy for emergencies.
- There are no expressway back-ups on the drive to work from Dad's house because it's mostly surface streets.
- I really know what's going on in my Dad's life.
- I'm getting to know my Dad's friends and neighbors.
- In Dad's circle of friends, I'm regarded as "the kid."
- The last time I ate this many meals with Dad I was a pre-teen.
- I know where all the decent fast food restaurants are between work and Dad's.
- I get to hear my Dad talk with his kids and end the conversations with "I love you."
- I've said "I love you" more times in the last five weeks than in the last five years. [I've been ending conversations with a "Love you" tag line so often that I almost ended a message to a coworker that way. At least I don't think I did....]

- I get to hear all of the history that my Dad knows.
- I know the broadcast times of all the conservative talk shows.
- I get to read the morning paper for free.
- I get my lunches packed for me.
- I go to bed at 10:05 p.m.
- I have to leave work on time—Dad expects me at six.
- My key chain sports two grocery-store value cards (so I can get bargains at my grocery store and Dad's).
- Gas is five cents a gallon cheaper in Dad's neighborhood.
- On long trips, we take Dad's car.
- I know what Vanna wore last night on *The Wheel*.
- I can now phrase all my answers in the form of questions. "What is: I've been watching way too much *Jeopardy!?*"
- The 76-degree air temperature in Dad's apartment is thinning down my blood in preparation for summer.
- The staff at the local pharmacy feels like family.
- I've discovered several gift-giving ideas for Dad…like new mattresses, new bedspreads, new pillows.
- I've learned that you can permanently readjust your spine by sleeping on a 25-year-old mattress bolstered with plywood.
- I've learned to be flexible… Appointments are merely rescheduling opportunities.
- And, finally, I've learned to live in the moment...
  ...What time is it? Seven o'clock? Gotta go.
     The Wheel is on.

P.S.   God bless all members of
         the sandwich generation.
         Remember—"Take one day
         at a time" and stock up
         on bread….

Young at heart

"Stay young!" he shouts through cupped hands to the musicians as they make their way out the door. "Thanks again, fellas, it was great!" he says, waving goodbye.

The band members smile and wave back, accepting the compliment they had worked hard to earn.

They had just finished an hour set of their best stuff for a rowdy, appreciative crowd. As they played the packed room, listeners clapped their hands, swayed to the beat, thumped on table tops, whistled the melody, and yelled "more, more" each time they came to a song's end.

The young-minded concert-goers grinned broadly and nodded warmly to each other as they joined in on familiar tunes: You Are My Sunshine, She'll be Comin' Round the Mountain, You Must Have Been a Beautiful Baby, Wabash Cannon Ball, Toot Toot Toostie, Five Foot Two, If You Knew Susie, My Darling Clementine, Yes Sir-That's My Baby, and Yankee Doodle Dandy.

The band a.k.a. "Three Men and Their Harmonicas" were the hit of the Saturday afternoon ice cream social. They cranked out tunes in rapid-fire succession without a break— except to take requests. They had more energy than most 35-year-olds, who I guessed to be about half their age.

The ice cream and music took place at The Marquette House, an assisted living residence—a hang-out for the "young at heart" who need a little help with daily living.

At The Marquette House, residents each have their own apartments and included in the rent are three square meals a day and an evening snack. Along with the food comes 24-hour emergency assistance, housekeeping, and daily planned activities like sing-alongs and ice cream socials.

It seems like the ideal domicile for a youthful guy like my Dad. We'll know soon. He moved in two weeks ago.

He lived in the old apartment for 25 years—with mom for the first dozen or so and on his own for the last half. He has lots of friends and was always spry and chipper. He was active at the senior center, calling bingo, sharing the "thought for the day," and telling jokes and stories to anyone who would listen. He was doing fine until about four months ago when he began to start feeling old and sad. His self-diagnosis: "I'm suffering from TMB—Too Many Birthdays!"

At 89, Dad does have some physical limitations and he's been depressed and lost his appetite, which led us to the conclusion that he couldn't live alone any longer. But, it wouldn't work to live with any of us. So, we decided on The Marquette House, which is just half a mile away from his old apartment building. That way he can stay in the same neighborhood and still get the services he needs.

His new, one bedroom apartment is bright and cheery with a beautiful view of the woods. And, in the living room, bedroom and bathroom there's an emergency pull chain in case he needs help from the staff.

Dad is settled now. He's got his car, his furniture, his clothes, his toiletries, his computer, and his keepsakes. He even has the same phone number.

We've done all we can do. Now, it's up to him.

Dad reports that the food is good and served in just the right portions for an elder statesman's appetite. And, it seems he eats his meals with a different group of women each day (even though there are plenty of men with whom he could keep mealtime company).

He's participated in The Marquette House version of Jeopardy! and Wheel Fortune. And, it's reported that he's been an avid participant in the current events discussions. He's even begun sharing jokes again.

Q.: "What did the astronauts say when they found the
bones on the moon?"
A.: "I guess the cow didn't make it!"

Kathy, the marketing director, refers to dad as "my Bill" and hints that they're looking for a bingo caller. While Peggy, the activity director has asked if Dad would like to begin sharing the thought for the day.

During the ice cream social, Dad enjoys a big bowl of vanilla ice cream with bananas, nuts, cherries, strawberries, and chocolate topping. We sit near the young, female staff member who's serving up the ice cream. Between mouthfuls, Dad's either teasing the female server or singing along with the band. At the end of each song, he yells through cupped hands, "More, more!"

After the ice cream social, Dad greets several staff members and residents by name. He thanks the band members "for a terrific performance" and we walk toward the reception desk in the lobby. As we approach the young woman sitting behind the desk, Dad introduces us. "This is Theresa," he says. "She has a wonderful laugh." Theresa blushes.

Then he motions for me to take a seat on the couch in the lobby. "Let's sit here for awhile and visit."

As we sit in the lobby, Dad sees somebody else he knows. Barbara and her father, Louie, stop by to talk. They were visiting Louie's sister who also lives in The Marquette House.

It seems Barbara fits Dad with his hearing aids and has for several years (ever since he decided that wearing his hearing aids helps him hear better!).

Dad tells Louie that his daughter is good at fitting hearing aids. Louie says, "I know," as he points to his two hearing aids. Barbara blushes and says thanks.

About that time, the band members walk by...

"Stay young!" Dad shouts through cupped hands to the musicians as they make their way out the door. "Thanks again, fellas, it was great!" he says, waving goodbye.

As I sit and watch Dad interact with old friends and new ones, with a renewed optimism, I think to myself,

Stay young, Dad. Stay young...

Note: There are many fine assisted living residences in the area. For details, contact your senior center or Area Agency on Aging.

A human life preserver

Two significant events happened in April 1912. The Titanic sunk and my father was born. You know about the Titanic—the unsinkable oceanliner—that sunk on its maiden voyage. But, you don't know about my father, the unsinkable Bill Powell.

Bill, now 89, is still afloat and helping others be the captains of their destiny. Let me explain.

When I was 24, my husband was unemployed and I needed to find a better job. During my job search, I found a position that paid twice what I was earning.

It was assistant to the director of a school job placement program. The job sounded interesting but required typing. I wanted to apply but didn't because I had poor typing skills.

One day soon after that, my father phoned. I mentioned the job I had seen. "What a neat opportunity, if only I could type."

My father said, "The important thing is you can spell and you know proper grammar, your typing will improve on the job. I think you should apply."

Armed with my father's faith and my resume, I applied for the job.

I failed the typing test, but they eventually hired me anyway. I've worked in education ever since.

A few years ago, I asked my father, "If you were me, would you have applied for that job?" To my shock, he answered, "No, but I had every confidence in you!"

It was then I realized how powerful words of encouragement can be. His encouragement gave me the strength to take a chance. His confidence enabled me to be successful—because I believed that he believed in me.

Like Bill, we can enable our family, friends, children, spouse, co-workers or boss.

How about spreading around some encouraging words? They just might help someone stay afloat in this sea of life.

Afterwords

Contact the following to learn more about...

Agriculture Tips/Animal Feed/Horse Supplies
Highland Feed and Water
217 E. Livingston
Highland, MI 48357
(248) 887-4100

Alzheimer's Disease
Alzheimer's Disease and
Related Disorders Association
919 North Michigan Avenue,
Suite 1100
Chicago, Illinois 60611-1676
(800) 272-3900
www.alz.org

American Business Women's Association
For Livingston CountyArea
Achates Charter Chapter/ABWA
P.O. Box 542
Howell, MI 48843
gallen48@juno.com

All others, contact:
National ABWA
9100 Ward Parkway
P.O. Box 8728
Kansas City, MO 64114-0728
(816) 361-6621
www.abwa.org

Bats
Bat Conservation International
P. O. Box 162603
Austin, Texas 78716-2603
(512) 327-9721
www.batcon.org

Pets for Adoption
Humane Society
of Livingston County
2464 Dorr Rd.
Howell, MI 48843
(517) 552-8050

Senior Citizen Issues
For southern and western
Wayne County
Area Agency on Aging 1-C
The Senior Alliance
3850 2nd Street, Suite 201
Wayne, MI 48184
(734) 722-2830

All others, contact:
National Elder Care Locator
(800) 677-1116
to locate your community's
Area Agency on Aging.

Attention Organizations and Groups:
Quantity discounts are available on bulk purchases of this book
for fund raising. For information, please contact:
Funny Farm, INK., P. O. Box 869, Highland, Michigan 48357